A Second Chance at Love

An erotic romance short story collection by
Michelle Houston

MICHELLE HOUSTON

MICHELLE HOUSTON

Trust

The first time around they
weren't ready. Now five
star-crossed couples get ...

A SECOND
CHANCE
AT *Love*

"a sexy read of love and trust"
~ Sensual Reads and Reviews

www.unleashedink.com

A SECOND CHANCE AT LOVE

Cover art © 2014 Michelle Lee
Edited by Jenna Byrnes and D. Musgrave

Published by Unleashed Ink

This book is dedicated to all those who found love the first time around; those who gave love a second (or third …) chance; and those who are still looking. Finding someone to spend your life with is hard … but worth it.

* * *

It goes without saying that in any writing endeavor, there are those that are behind the scenes that make writing possible. To all who have assisted me along the way - thank you.

A special note of appreciate to D. Musgrave and Jenna Brynes for hours of editing and critiquing, as well as friendship. You two have kept me grounded when I was lost in the clouds, and offered shoulders to cry on, when I needed it.

To Gail Roughton for her assistance with cover art concepts - this cover rocks because of your help!

To Connie for her beta reading … support and encouragement.

And to my husband - who supports me even when my characters scare him a little bit - my heartfelt thanks and love. Without him, these stories would never have been written. Especially *Diggin' Up Bones* - which he tore apart, and helped me rebuild.

TABLE OF CONTENTS:

MICHELLE HOUSTON

Diggin' Up Bones

A SECOND CHANCE AT LOVE

DIGGIN UP BONES
Chapter One

Alisa took a sip of coffee and leaned forward, putting her elbows on the edge of the sink, and looked out the window. Wisps of red hair escaped her ponytail and she tucked the free strands behind her ear as she watched people scurrying around outside in her backyard, rudely disturbing what would have been a quiet spring morning.

"Great, just great," she muttered, turning away and heading down the hall to her study. Just as she was about to enter, a knock sounded at her front door. Cradling her cup in both hands, she went to the door and opened it.

The bane of her existence, all six feet two inches of him, stood there. Zach Bradford, part time archeologist, full time pain in the ass. Not in the mood to be polite, she stood and stared at him, impatiently waiting for him to tell her why he was further ruining her day. It would help if she hated him, but hate was the farthest thing from her mind when she was around him. Despite her best efforts, just looking at him made her melt inside.

"It's just like we thought."

Despite her thoughts, Alisa couldn't help but respond to his voice. Like whiskey, it was deep with an edge to it that gave it a kick.

"The finger bones and hatchet head you found are Native American. The testing confirmed it. They've also found some pottery shards and a leg bone so far today. It's looking as if we'll be here a while."

Without saying a word, Alisa nodded and tried to close the door, but Zach stopped it with his foot. Glaring at him, she gave the door a push. "I've said you can do your dig. Now go!"

"Alisa, I--"

Her eyes closed at the pain his words caused. Despite the years, she remembered the phrase that had started out the same way so long ago. *'Alisa, I love you, talk to me, please. What's going on?'* But she hadn't been able to tell him her secret shame. She hadn't been able to tell anyone.

He continued, "I didn't mean for this to happen. But you know, as well as I do, any Native American artifacts found have to be preserved. The Cherokee Nation's representative will be here soon to begin overseeing the dig and the preservation of any items retrieved."

Opening her eyes, she fought to keep calm. "I'm aware of that, Zach, that's why I called you! I told you I'd support your dig on my property. What more do you want from me?" Despite her best efforts, she could hear the pain that laced each word. She knew Zach would hear it, too.

"I just want us to be friends again."

Good ol' Zach, everybody's buddy. Even after she pushed him away, he had tried to remain her friend. The annual birthday and Christmas cards he sent her like clockwork testified to that fact. It was the other gifts, the treasured book on Valentine's Day, sent by messenger and without a card, the single red rose delivered on the anniversary of their first date, and the dozens of other little things that he anonymously sent to her that let her know he was still in love with her. And it all nearly broke her heart.

As much as she hated to do it, she had to be firm. She wasn't ready for him yet--and didn't know if she ever would be. She loved him too much to ask him to wait.

"I don't think we can be friends. Now, if you don't mind, I have some work to do." As he pulled his foot back, Alisa gently closed the door and locked it. Leaning against the heavy wood, she allowed the tears to flow. So many years and so much wasted time. Smacking her palm against the door in frustration, she slowly slid down to the floor and brought her knees up against her chest.

It was so unfair. She had just started pulling her life back together, back to the point that she had considered dating again.

She needed to find a nice, non-threatening man first, someone who was as opposite from Zach as she could get. Setting his height aside, he was the most physically overwhelming person she knew. His striking features gave silent testimony to his partial Native American heritage and captured feminine attention instantly. His hands--she shivered just thinking about them. So firm, with calluses from farm work and his digs, just rough enough to lightly abrade her skin. His strong, broad shoulders begged a woman to curl up against him and let him shelter her from all the world's problems.

Laughing softly and without humor, Alisa admitted that was part of the problem. If she had told him, he would have smothered her, trying to fix it all for her. She feared he might even have killed for her, if it came down to it.

Catching her reflection in the hall mirror, she shuddered at the haunted look in her blue eyes. Closing them, she shoved back the memories that vied for her attention. Her breath hitched from the effort. Trying to focus on something else, she called to mind the image of Zach standing in her doorway, hands in his back pockets, with a smudge of dirt on his cheek. Her hands had itched to brush it away, to feel the heat of his skin against hers.

When they'd first met almost three years before, he had been standing the same way. Covered in dirt and mud, with a breathtakingly handsome smile on his face, he had caught her attention instantly. She had tried to fight the attraction since he was five years older and already had his Bachelors degree while she was just starting her only year of college. He had a path planned for his life. She was just getting over the grief of losing her beloved grandparents, settling into the home they had left her, and trying to figure out what she wanted to do with her life.

* * *

Several hours later, she admitted defeat. She simply wasn't going to get any work done. Despite her best efforts, her gaze kept returning to the window and the man who stood outside, directing everyone around the dig. What she had planned to be her vegetable garden was now a gaping hole in the ground with a huge

9

canvas tent over it, blocking the sun from the two dozen or so people working there.

It didn't help that each of those workers took turns tromping through her house to use the restroom. Each knock meant she had to answer the door, wait patiently while the worker used the facilities, and then let them out again. Then she would close the door, head back down the hall to her study, and try to find her train of thought again.

Even with such limited contact, she could perceive the excitement as everyone carefully worked to uncover a brief hint of the past. Under different circumstances, she would have been out there with them, getting everyone drinks, if nothing else. But Zach was present.

It was her own fault, really. If she'd gone to someone else when she uncovered the bones, she would have saved herself a world of heartache and a headache that no amount of Tylenol would cure. But she'd gone to the one man she knew she could trust, the one man she should have avoided at all costs. With his heritage and his strong sense of community, Zach would work to preserve the bones and any artifacts found. She could sleep safe, knowing that nothing would be stolen while he was running the dig, but she still wasn't able to sleep. He kept interrupting her dreams. He was persistent, just as he had been in getting her to consider going out with him.

For weeks, she had turned him down, always with a soft smile and the hope he would ask again. And sure enough, every few days, he would. Until finally she agreed to go out with him.

The look on his face at that moment was one she would always remember. Shock and happiness meshed with a hint of smoldering male desire.

As if he knew she was thinking about him, he looked up from where he knelt on the ground working on some task with one of his crew. His gaze met hers through the window. Despite the passing of nearly two years, she found him just as attractive as he had been in college. Sun-kissed skin, thick and vibrant chestnut brown hair, and blue eyes so pale they seemed eerie at times. He was what many women would consider gorgeous. Hell, he was what she would consider gorgeous, and had for many years. Even now, her pulse raced a little faster and he wasn't even in the same room with her.

Everyone had always commented on how well they complimented each other. Him with his rugged, striking features and her with what Zach always called a 'lush and sensual build'. To him, she was a redheaded Marilyn Monroe. But she didn't feel so sensual now, and hadn't since the last time she had kissed him.

It didn't help that she had lost a lot of weight in the long months since she had last seen him.

Unable, or willing, to deal with the longings that flooded her, she turned away. She crossed the study, heading to her bedroom while trying to deny her reaction to him. Even trusting him as she did with the dig, she didn't know if she could bring herself to trust him--or any man for that matter--with her body.

Outside she heard the sounds of the crew packing up for the day. Grabbing a change of clothes, she headed into the bathroom. She turned on the taps in the shower, set the temperature to just below scalding, and shed her clothes. While she waited for the water to heat up, she turned and looked at herself in the bathroom mirror. Although of medium height for a woman, her lush curves had always been an issue for her. Men tended to see the body and ignore her intelligence. She wasn't a knock out or classically beautiful, but she wasn't a toad either. Only Zach had ever made her feel like he saw the real woman inside, admiring her brain as well as her curves.

Her emotions in a whirlwind, as they had been for the last week, she stepped under the shower spray and prayed for it to sooth her tattered nerves.

She had to give Zach credit, though. Whenever someone got too close to the house, he directed them somewhere else, trying to keep everyone together and as quiet as possible. He knew she needed quiet time to write. He'd always understood about her writing time and about so many other things, especially her virginity and her fears about losing it. He had been so patient, waiting for the right time. But it had never arrived for them.

The water washed away her frustrations and beat at her tight muscles. She leaned back against the cool tiles and closed her eyes, allowing her hands free reign. Of their own volition, they cupped her breasts, holding the slight weight in their palms as her fingers

11

rolled her tight nipples. She lost herself in fantasy. Zach was under the spray with her, his rough, work calloused hands holding her breasts, teasing her nipples with his thumbs as his lips pressed soft kisses along her throat.

Gliding a hand down her stomach, she paused at her belly button, tracing over the sensitive little valley, then continued. Slipping a finger past her pouting lips and dipping it into her moist core, she stroked the sensitive skin. She had been wet ever since she'd watched Zach walk across her lawn earlier, the rising sun hitting his hair just enough to bring out the deep chestnut with its natural highlights. Long-legged, his strides had eaten up the earth as he moved with purpose. He mingled with the crew, often gesturing with his hands to make his point. A fluid grace filled his movements and her body remembered well being the recipient of his caresses.

Thrusting her finger deep, she rubbed her thumb over her clit, desperately trying to take the edge off her frustrations.

Zach's presence just outside her house had her emotions in turmoil, and it was only getting worse. She had almost leaned forward and kissed him at the door, she wanted his touch so badly. Just watching each of his words form on his lips had aroused her. Topped with his voice as he spoke, it had taken all her will power to turn away from him. It didn't help that despite not knowing why she'd pushed him away, he still wanted her. She saw it in his blue eyes every time he looked at her. It seemed time hadn't lessened what they felt for each other, as she had hoped. The rate it was going, a decade could go by and she would still melt into a puddle when he walked into the room.

Alternating her hand from one breast to the other, she teased and pinched her nipples while she manipulated her clit and pussy with the other. Her legs grew weak as her inner muscles tightened, trying to milk a cock that wasn't there.

Locking her legs tight, she arched her back against the shower wall as tremors raced through her. Mouth open, she gasped for air. Her insides were on fire, and in her mind's eye it was Zach's fingers driving her wild, his fingers slowly thrusting in and out of her pussy while his mouth plundered hers.

With a soft cry, a shudder wracking her body, she climaxed. Her essence leaked down her hand to wash away in the torrents of water racing down her body from the showerhead. Gasping softly, she dropped to her knees, her legs too weak to hold her. Tipping her head into the spray, she flipped her hair over her shoulder and let the water wash away her tears, as they streamed from her eyes.

The emptiness of not having Zack's arms to hold her as she cried returned, along with the horrible, terrifying memory of another man holding her down, violating her.

DIGGIN UP BONES
Chapter Two

Whatever soft feelings she'd harbored for Zach the night before were gone now. If his crew bellowed one more time, she was going to go out there and kill him with her bare hands. Then she'd kick his people off her land and finish the damn dig herself. At least then, she would be able to enjoy the peace and quiet that living outside of the city limits was supposed to afford.

Frustrated, she slapped her hand against her desk. She gave serious thought to creating a character modeled after him, just so she could kill him off in a slow, painful manner. And the character would deserve every moment of it.

"Hey Zach, check this out," someone yelled outside.

"That's it!" Pushing her chair back, Alisa stood and moved around the desk. After her inability to write the day before, she'd turned her desk around in hopes that it would give her a little more peace. However, as she banged her hip and had to squeeze past it to get out of the room, it only frustrated her more. And as irrational as she knew it to be, she wanted to kick Zach for that, too.

Stomping down the hall, she reached the back door and thrust it open. Several pairs of eyes widened as she stepped outside for the first time since the crew had arrived. Storming past several surprised workers, she crossed her lawn and walked right up behind the man she was quickly coming to suspect was trying to drive her insane.

Jabbing him in the shoulder with an extended index finger, she demanded his attention. When he spun around, she noted with satisfaction the guilty look on his chiseled face. "I thought you said you were going to make every effort to be quiet!"

He raised his hands, reaching for her upper arms. At the touch of his skin against hers, her body awakened, need flooding her. She wanted to step closer, to press tight against him. Jerking away, she took a step back, before her body betrayed her. "You promised me that you were all going to keep the shouting to a minimum and do all the heavy machinery work in the morning, and do the quieter parts in the afternoon. So far today, you've been screamed at five times! And every time, it's been by someone standing right outside my window!"

Alisa knew her voice was getting shrill and that everyone had to think she was insane. But her writing was the one thing she had any real control over. And they were taking it away from her bit by painful bit with each loud shout.

"Alisa, please calm down." Zach took a step closer and lowered his voice. "I know you're frustrated by all this and I promise I'll have a talk with my crew about their noise levels when they're near the house."

Still frustrated and breathing heavily, Alisa became aware of everyone's eyes on her--so many eyes, staring at her, judging her. Lifting a hand to her lips in embarrassment at her actions, she spun away and hurried back inside. Zach rushed after her, calling her name. She slammed the door in his face and locked the deadbolt.

Zach stood on the other side of the door seemingly for ages, softly knocking, his husky voice asking her to open the door. God, how she wanted to. Rubbing her hands over her arms where he had so briefly touched her, she bit back a sob. She craved his touch more then ever, but she wasn't strong enough to reach out for him.

Zach was so intense, so willing to take charge. All it would take was a quick flick of the lock and a twist of the doorknob. She wouldn't even have to open the door; just unlocking it would be enough. Zach would do the rest. He would pull her against him, hold her in his arms, his lips would press against hers, and life would make sense again. It would be so easy to end the torment she was putting herself through. But the thought of taking that step, opening herself up to him, especially after working so hard to push him away, terrified her. She wasn't sure if she was ready, or if she was only holding herself back out of habit.

So many times over the last two years, she had wanted to tell him the truth--that she loved him so much there were times it seemed she couldn't breathe. That she had been violated. That his intensity overwhelmed her.

Maybe if she hadn't allowed her fears about pregnancy or rushing things to keep her from losing her virginity to him, then it wouldn't be such a frightening idea. But despite her fantasies, regardless of all the erotica she had read, the fact remained that the only experience she had was a brutal attack which had left her broken for longer than she cared to remember.

She trusted Zach, more than anyone alive. But she had trusted the man who raped her, too. She had believed he was her friend; that he only wanted to give her a ride home.

She knew in her heart that Zach would never hurt her, but the fragile part of her mind, the part created that summer night two years before as her supposed friend dragged her out of his car and forced himself on her, screamed that she had trusted him, too.

As the patterns of light and shadow reflecting through the glass pane on the door shifted, she heard the soft tread of Zach's work boots moving across the porch and down the stairs. Folding her arms over her waist, the weight of her conflicting need for Zach and her anguish at what had been taken from her--from both of them--crushed her.

Unable to hold back the tears, she cried so hard her body shook with it. Overwhelmed, she rushed down the hallway to her bedroom. Flinging herself on the bed, she curled on her side around the stuffed wolf cub Zach had given her on their third date. Torturing herself with impossible daydreams of what could have been, she fell into a broken sleep.

* * *

Later that evening, when the last of the digging crew had gone home for the night, Alisa opened her front door and let the breeze in. While the coffee pot percolated, she settled into her porch swing and enjoyed the music of the night. All around her crickets and locusts called out for their mates, performing such sweet melodies. A light breeze carried the sounds of the horses in her neighbors' pasture as they whinnied faintly in the night air.

So lost in the beauty of nature, she didn't hear the light footsteps coming around her porch until Zach stood beside her. Fighting the urge to bolt inside, Alisa gripped the arm of her swing until her knuckles turned white. She wanted to run to him, to flee into the familiarity of her house, but forced herself to do neither and remain where she was.

"I thought you'd left." Whisper-soft, her voice trembled as Zach settled beside her, his long legs spread out before him. He was only a breath away from touching her. All she had to do was shift slightly, and she would be pressed against him from shoulder to hip to ankle.

"I did. Ares needed some exercise and I was worried about you. So we rode back to check on you." As if choreographed, his horse chose that moment to poke his head around the corner, searching for grass to munch on.

"Why?" Alisa wanted to shy away from him, even as the urge to reach out and hold his hand ate at her. Honeysuckle gave a light fragrance to the air, while the crickets created a soothing symphony. Zach's intense personality was leashed, but just barely. The evening was almost too perfect.

"I know we're disturbing you with the dig, but I didn't realize how much until today. I'm sorry. I can cut back the number of people in the crew, which should cut down the noise, but it will also take longer to finish. I tried to work a balance out, but I guess I misjudged."

"It's not that." Unspoken were the words that she knew would hurt him. It's you. She couldn't say them; she'd already hurt him enough.

"Then what is it?"

Damn him! He couldn't leave well enough alone. Ever. For weeks after she broke up with him, he'd stopped by her house, convinced that she didn't mean it. And why would he since he had no way of knowing her reasons. She knew it hadn't helped that no one knew what was going on, not her friends, and certainly not Zach. She hadn't even gone to the hospital, too ashamed to tell anyone.

"I should head inside." She moved to stand. His warm hand laid over hers, holding her still. If he'd put any pressure on it, she would have bolted. But just that light touch was enough to hold her captive. He'd always been like that, aware of the differences in their builds and ever so careful of his strength. But his eyes had given him away. So light, they brimmed with desire every time he had looked at her, and he had never hidden how his body reacted to her presence.

"Ares misses you, you know."

She gave a jerky nod as the memory of flying across the pasture on the stallion surfaced. Zach racing behind her on his gelding's back, not quite able to catch up. She had thrown back her head and laughed as she reached her yard, then pulled Ares to a halt to wait on Zach. He had dismounted and pulled her down into his arms. They had dropped to the ground and wrestled, rolling around kissing, while the horses wandered away to munch on the grass, much as Ares was doing now. Ruthlessly, she shoved the memory away.

"What happened with us, Alisa? I know it's ancient history, but I think I deserve an answer. I've wondered often over the last two years what I did to drive you away. Then out of the blue, you come to me, telling me you didn't know who else to trust, and just like that you're in my life again. So many times, I have reached out--and nothing. Not a card, email, or even a form letter. Even forwarded chain mail would have been something. Christ." He ran a hand through his hair, ruffling the silken strands.

Her heart lurched at the hurt in his voice. She desperately wanted to tell him, to try to explain her actions, but her throat closed up. The naked pain on his face as he looked at her was enough to bring tears to her eyes. She had been hurt by the attack, but so had he. She was just coming to realize how much.

"Even after all this time, just the sight of you, or the smell of your perfume, makes me tremble." He held out the hand he had just run through his hair.

Shaky herself, Alisa lifted her hand to his face, cupping his square jaw in her palm. His five o'clock shadow rasped against her fingers. Closing her eyes, she remembered the sensation of his lips pressing against her neck, his whiskers coarse on her skin.

He moved closer, and she trembled with the knowledge he was going to kiss her. She was so afraid that she'd feel trapped. But when his lips briefly brushed against hers, she found herself melting against him. Pulling her hand free of his, she lifted it to his chest and pressed it over his heart as he deepened the kiss.

Old longings merged with new desires. She parted her lips, allowing his tongue entrance. Beneath her palm, his heart raced. It was like her first kiss, and yet it wasn't. They had kissed before, many times over the months they had dated. But it was the first since her rape; the first time she'd trusted someone enough to let him get close.

Her own heart racing, Alisa pulled back. Lifting her gaze shyly to meet his, she saw desire in his eyes. His nostrils flared as he took a deep breath.

"You still love me, don't you?" His voice caught, betraying his vulnerability. Despite the pain she had caused him, her answer mattered. He still loved her. And heaven help her, it was the truth, she still loved him so much her heart threatened to rip in two.

Uncertain what to say, Alisa worried at her bottom lip. As his gaze dropped to follow the motion, she stood, her hand still pressed against his face.

"Yes," she whispered and allowed her fingers to slowly trail over his lips, tracing the firmness of them. "I always have. I think I always will."

Zach watched her back away, a strange light in his eyes. If she hadn't known better, she'd think that he knew her secret. But that wasn't possible. No one knew.

Her gaze still locked on Zach's, she stepped inside and closed the door--once again shutting him out. Moments passed in tense silence as she stood with held breath, waiting for Zach to come after her, even as she feared what would happen if he did.

She exhaled in a rush at the sound of him retreating. Ares whinnied, and looking out the window, Alisa could see Zach mount him and turn the stallion around, heading across the yard. Pressing her palm against the glass, her heart aching, she waited for him to look back. Just as she was giving up hope, Ares stopped and Zach shifted in the saddle.

The moonlight cast his face in shadows, but she knew he saw her standing there. He lifted his hand, as if to wave, then abruptly dropped it. Turning back around in the saddle, he tapped the reins and Ares galloped off. Alisa watched him until he went around the corner, disappearing from sight.

DIGGIN UP BONES
Chapter Three

The next few days passed quietly but slowly. Gradually, the number of people on the dig dwindled, until nearly a week after her blow up, Alisa could see from her study window only a dozen or so people milling about. Many of them often stopped to say hi or mention what they had uncovered as they headed into her house to use the bathroom. Each time, she felt a little more comfortable responding, until by the end of the fourth day, she headed outside with a tray of refreshments. Most of the workers swarmed over to her, eager to drink anything out of a glass, rather than a bottle.

Zach's assistant, a spunky young up-and-comer who made her wonder what Zach had been like when he was an undergraduate, was the hardest to win over. After the first bout of refreshments, he wandered off, glass in hand. While chatting with several other workers, she overheard him ask another guy if he thought "the drinks were laced with arsenic."

Smothering a laugh, she withdrew from her conversation and headed over towards him. She waited until he had swallowed the last drop of his lemonade, then held out her hand and said, "It's actually hemlock."

As his eyes bugged, she allowed the laugh to escape, catching Zach's attention. The beast had the audacity to wink at her before he turned his attention back to carefully brushing what they suspected was another bone fragment.

As the days drifted past, she continued to bring drinks out every few hours, making sure to note who seemed to prefer what beverage, and tried to stay out of Zach's way. He, on the other hand, was doing his best to drive her steadily insane. He was nothing short of kind and considerate. Yet it seemed he used every excuse he could think up to stop what he was doing when she came outside. Not that she could call him on it, as everyone on the dig stopped their own tasks.

To make matters worse, he was waging a sensual war on her. He would 'accidentally' brush up against her, or he'd hand her something and their fingers would touch, and he never failed to press a brief kiss against the top of her head before she headed back inside. Sometimes, he would brush his hand over the small of her back or her hip, and she could experience the heat of his skin through her clothing. Those touches she liked the most. Her arousal soared, building with each touch--which she suspected was his plan--until she thought she was going to go insane with her hunger.

After their one brief kiss, he hadn't tried again. She found herself licking her lips when they talked or worrying her bottom lip between her teeth. But despite the sudden flares of heat in his eyes, Zach didn't try to kiss her. Even as she appreciated his patience as she worked things out, she wanted to smack him. She had done everything she could think of, everything that had always provoked him to kiss her before, save either kiss him herself or ask to be kissed. And he still hadn't.

Shaking off her mood, she set the tray of empty glasses down on the table and headed down to her study to get back to work on her latest novel. She was behind on her schedule and if she didn't hurry, she'd never meet her deadline.

Most of the day passed as quietly as her morning. Her only real problem was getting her car out of her driveway to go to the grocery store. But Zach's assistant, the same undergrad student who feared a few days before that she was trying to poison them all, quickly solved her problem. Instead of rounding everyone up to move their cars so she could get out, he handed her the keys to his.

Switching off Randy Travis as he crooned from the radio about "resurrecting memories of a love that's dead and gone", she drove to town in silence, alone with her thoughts. She'd allowed herself to become a victim of something she had no say in and had pushed Zach away as a result. Now that Zach was back in her life and seemed willing to stay, she wanted to stop being a victim and go after him.

Her mind made up, she pulled into the grocery store parking lot and into a slot. Inside, she finished her shopping as quickly as she could and headed to the pharmacy section.

Her nerve almost gave out as she saw the plethora of condoms that were available. She was uncertain if "ribbed for her pleasure" was better than simple latex, or if Zach would prefer a sensitive one over extra spermicidal. Looking at the size options, her eyes crossed. Not about to give up, she closed her eyes and grabbed a box at random. Without looking at it, she tossed it into her cart and headed to the checkout.

The cashier raised an eyebrow when she saw the chosen condoms. Glancing down, Alisa saw why. Instead of a simple three pack, she'd grabbed a twelve pack. She read, Extra sensitive, for his pleasure, on the front of the box. At that moment, she wished the ground would open up and swallow her whole.

Before she could back out, she tossed the rest of her purchases on the belt and looked away towards the gum, waiting for the total to be rung up. Utterly mortified by the time she left the store, she almost flung the condoms in the trash. Only the memory of Zach's lips against hers stopped her.

She was tired of being a victim, and each time she pulled back from what she wanted, she was letting her attacker remain in control. It was enough that she'd been too immature and scared to press charges. She refused to let him rule her life anymore; she wasn't going to continue to give him that power over her.

She was a full-grown woman and there was nothing--*nothing*--wrong with her having sex. Having a sexual drive was healthy and normal; it was the last few years of living afraid of her own desires that wasn't. It had taken her a while to reach that conclusion, and she wasn't about to back out now.

She was going to seduce Zach Bradford.

* * *

She pulled the borrowed car into her driveway and Zach turned from talking to one of his workers, his head lifting and his pale gaze flowing over her. Abruptly ending his conversation, he walked toward her, his long legs quickly carrying him across her lawn to her driveway. Alisa hopped out and grabbed the bag with the condoms before he arrived, shoving it down inside her bathroom bag, which had such lovely things as toilet paper and shower gel.

"Need a hand?"

Nodding her head, she grabbed a few bags and stepped back, letting him get the rest. With her hip, she pushed the door closed.

"Lead the way."

Aware of his eyes on her, Alisa added an extra degree of wiggle to her walk. From the sharply indrawn breath and stifled groan behind her, she knew she'd achieved the desired effect. He was definitely still interested and now he knew she was, too.

She climbed the steps of her porch, and while juggling her bags and keys, she managed to open the back door and move into the kitchen. Tossing her keys on the table as she passed, she stopped at the counter and set her bags down. Zach brushed against her as he moved to her side, setting the rest down on the floor at her feet. She felt his gaze trailing up her body as he slowly stood straight.

"I thought maybe you might like to stay for dinner tonight," she stammered, her stomach fluttering from the heat of his gaze.

A soft, sensual smile curled his lips. She almost swooned as his dimples winked at her. "I'd love to."

"Good. Um, it's not going to be anything fancy, just a steak and salad, but..."

Zach lifted a hand to her lips, pressing a finger to silence her. "Steak sounds good. I happen to like steak. Remember?"

Alisa nodded as her wicked juices started bubbling. Pursing her lips, she pressed a kiss against his finger before parting them and sucking the tip into her mouth. Passion flared in his eyes, and an answering awareness awakened within her.

His gaze locked on hers, Zach pulled his finger away and tipped his head down, pressing his lips to hers. Alisa closed her eyes and lost herself in his embrace. His hands, always so steady, trembled when he lightly took her arms and pulled her against his chest. She clung to him, helpless to do anything except drown in his kiss.

She was lost in a sensual void, drowning in emotions she'd dreamed about--fantasized about--for so long. And now she was experiencing it. It was explosive compared to the yearning of her previous self, the nineteen-year-old college student with her first real love. Her breasts ached for his touch. Her nipples tightened, forming hard pebbles against the soft cotton of her bra.

Zach was her rock, anchoring her in the maelstrom of sensations his touch had awakened. She wanted him with a fierceness that shook her. She had read about it, but never imagined that it could be anything like the authors described. She felt like she was flying and drowning at the same time. Pulling him in tighter, she deepened the kiss. She wasn't going to debate what she was doing, if she was ready for it. She was going to let her heart take charge for once.

With a groan against her lips, Zach broke the kiss. Gently, he pulled her arms from around his neck and stepped back, breathing heavily. Alisa startled as she realized her breath was just as unsteady.

Running his hands through her vibrant red hair, he smoothed her long bangs back from her face. Zach whispered, regret tightening his voice, "I have to get back to work before they come looking for me."

Alisa nodded in agreement. "Yeah, that wouldn't be good." She licked her lips, quivering inside as his gaze tracked the motion of her tongue.

"But I'll be back once they've left. We need to talk, baby, as much as I know you don't want to."

"Yeah," she whispered. "I think we do." As much as she didn't want to, she was going to have to tell him. He deserved to know before they went any further.

With that thought in mind, she set about getting everything ready for the evening ahead. She made it through showering and shaving, the trial of deciding what to wear, pulled on panties and a robe for modesty's sake, and was in the middle of changing the sheets on her bed when it hit her. She was going to seduce Zach, or at the very least, let him seduce her.

Her heart beat faster and her body reacted to the pictures floating through her mind. Untying her robe, she pushed the edges aside and cupped her breasts, running her thumbs over her nipples before she pinched the hard buds. Shrugging off the robe, she stood in the middle of her bedroom and looked at herself in the mirror while she slid her hands over her body. The image reflected back at her was so much like her younger self, bubbling with repressed sensuality and fully aware of it.

Smiling softly, she started sliding her hands over her stomach and thighs, while her mirrored image did the same. She just wished it was Zach's hands gliding over her, his lips pressing against her neck as he awakened her body.

She let her hand slide down her panties, softly stroking her clit, enjoying mental images of the possible night to come, when someone outside started calling for some help.

Suddenly aware of how carried away she had gotten, Alisa pulled her hand from her panties and turned her focus once more to the bed, after licking her cream from her finger. As much as her body screamed for an orgasm, she wanted to wait--her next one should be with Zach.

DIGGIN UP BONES
Chapter Four

When Zach knocked on the screen door later that evening, Alisa had to bite the inside of her mouth to hold back her laughter. His hair was in wild disarray, giving him a mad scientist look. Topping off his wild hair was a streak of dirt along one cheek, which reached from his hairline, down the side of his face, and curled toward his nose. Her fingers itched to trace the sharp line of his cheekbone, to trail down the thin blade of his nose, brushing the dirt away with soft caresses. His clothes were another matter. Not just mildly dirty--he was filthy. Her heart lurched at the remembrance that when they first met he had been the same way. It seemed fitting.

"Mind if I take a quick shower? I have my gym clothes with me." The gym bag he held in his hand appeared to be the only part of him not covered in dirt.

Barely holding her laughter in check, Alisa nodded and stepped back. Pointing down the hallway, she hoped she remembered to close her bedroom door. As he walked out of the room, she caught a glimpse of the back of his clothing and that sealed it. A spurt of laughter escaped, making him spin on his heels. "What's so funny?"

"You," she retorted, mirth lacing her words. "You're filthy!"

"Well darlin', we always knew I'd grow up to be a dirty old man some day. I'm just getting a head start on the dirty part." His good ol' boy drawl did nothing to hide the laughter lighting up his own eyes.

"Go on, get your shower. Dinner's almost ready."

Turning back to the stove, she did her best to ignore the sounds of him moving about in her bathroom. For a moment, she wondered in horror if she had left her dirty clothes lying out from her shower, but remembered that they were in the laundry room just before she tried to sneak in and get them.

Moments later, when the sound of the shower reached her ears, a mental image of Zach standing under the spray shot into her mind's eye. She pictured his bronze skin being pelted with tiny droplets of water. A bolt of lust hit her so hard she dropped her salad tongs. Cursing under her breath, she bent and picked them up, then tossed them in the sink. She wondered if his chest was still hairless, hinting at his Native American ancestry. It was one of the reasons she had brought the bones to him when she found them. She had known there was a real possibility they were Native American, and that he would protect the dig, even if he drove her crazy in the process.

But she was coming to realize there had been another reason, one she hadn't been aware of at the time. She wanted him back in her life. The desire to be with anyone else just wasn't there, even though she had told herself she must be ready to start dating again. Subconsciously, she knew she had used the find as an excuse to let him back into her life, and other than the disruption to her routines, she hadn't regretted it.

The sounds of his voice singing caught her by surprise. Alisa strained to hear what he was singing but couldn't tell. All she caught was the deep rumble of his voice mingling with the sounds of water in the pipes. She remembered when he used to sing to her while they sat on her porch swing, listening to the crickets at night. Husky with emotion, he would sing softly while holding her against his chest, his fingers running through her hair. Occasionally, he'd steal a kiss or caress her softly. Sometimes it had been innocent, a brush of his knuckles along her neck, the soft glide of his hands against her hips. Other times, he would gently cup her breasts while he kissed her or pulled her tight against him, so that his erection pressed against her.

After a couple of months, he had hinted that he was ready to take things further, but she had held back. Sheltered for most of her life, she had been scared of what she was feeling. Scared that in the heat of the moment they would get caught up and forget to protect themselves, that she would ruin his hard work by getting pregnant before they were ready. Now regret for that lost time filled her. It would have been so sweet, losing her virginity to him. He would have made it perfect.

Her fears had caused her to balk at giving her virginity to Zach, only to have it taken from her by someone she considered a friend. She hadn't seen him since that night, but he continued to have power over her. Now, she was through letting the memory of him haunt her.

Shaking her head to clear it of the fog of the past, she turned off the burner and moved the steaks from the skillet onto plates, then grabbed an oven mitt to pull the baked potatoes from the oven. She heard the shower turn off as she worked on dividing their salads into bowls. She was just getting their food on the table, when he entered the room.

Lust slammed into her, hard and heavy, as she caught sight of his bare skin. His 'gym clothes' consisted of a pair of cotton shorts and a sleeveless shirt that showed off every inch of his tanned arms.

"Smells good."

All she could manage was a nod and hoped her tongue wasn't hanging out of her mouth. As Zach walked past her to the other side of the table, he paused and pressed a quick kiss against her lips.

The man had to know what he was doing to her. There was no way he couldn't. He was driving her insane on purpose. She was either going to spontaneously combust or find herself committed to the asylum if she didn't act soon.

"You going to sit down?" he asked with a grin, his dimples drawing her attention. Feeling the heat of a blush staining her cheeks, she pulled out her chair and sat down, turning her attention to her plate.

They ate in companionable silence. Occasionally he'd take her hand and brush his thumb along the ridge of her knuckles, or his long legs would brush against hers under the table. It became a challenge to keep from moaning at the sensations he evoked within her. She knew her panties were already damp, just waiting for the right moment when his cock slid into her, filling the empty place within her.

She was just about done with her food when she looked up and caught Zach staring at her. Self-conscious, she licked at the corner of her mouth, checking to see if food was clinging there. "What?"

Zach smiled and shook his head. "Nothing. I was just watching you eat, that's all." He reached across the table and took her hand in his, giving her a gentle squeeze before turning his attention back to his plate.

Unable to handle the unexpected tense silence, Alisa asked, "So, how's the dig going? I hope you're finding something."

Zach nodded as he finished chewing a bite of steak. "Yep. Just today we've found a few more pottery shards, and what we are wagering is a finger bone of a female. We're still waiting on some results from a few other items we found in the last few days, and we have a few more sections of the grid that we plan to search. All in all, it's been a successful find."

Uncertain what to say, Alisa settled for nodding and murmuring "uh huh" softly. Zach's dimples flashed as his smile deepened.

"So, I've been meaning to ask, how many of my crew have you killed off so far?"

Alisa's head jerked up. For a moment, she wondered if he was serious, if someone had mentioned her run in with his assistant, and the whole arsenic joke.

"I figure by now, I've died about a dozen times, and each of my crew has been the model for one, maybe two, characters."

She laughed softly, remembering doing just that. She had killed him off closer to two dozen times. Several were very inventive, although she wasn't about to tell him that.

"Um, just a few. One of your crew created the perfect character. He's got bright purple hair, tattoos on both arms, wire rimmed glasses, and a subdued and serious attitude one minute, then he's joking and cutting up the next."

Zach smiled, the planes of his face softening. "That would be my assistant, Trevor. You borrowed his car today, as a matter of fact."

"Yeah. Never would have pictured him listening to country, not with the gothic look he is trying to cultivate."

Sitting across from him, it seemed like old times, when they would enjoy dinner at his apartment. She could remember as if it was yesterday, their last steak dinner. She had just gotten the acceptance letter on her first novel, and he had splurged on thick steaks, so tender she could almost cut it with her fork.

Afterwards, they had sat on his couch and cuddled, and she had almost allowed him to seduce her.

"Speaking of characters, how are things going with the book?"

"Good, for the most part. I still have some catching up to do, and my characters don't want to cooperate with the outline I have planned for them, but it's wrapping up nicely. I also have an idea for another book forming in the back of my mind. It involves magic and a taboo ritual. In fact, if you're willing, I might need your help with some of the research."

"I'd gladly help, you know that. But I get a signed copy of the book in payment."

"Deal." Just imagining the time she would be spending with him made her tremble. The pouring over old texts and research into Native American culture, so that she could create a fake tribe and still have it based in reality, would put them together for days, if not weeks.

She already knew he would take every opportunity to stand behind her and lift her hair up off her neck so that he could kiss the nape of her neck softly. She caught herself closing her eyes as the vivid image sprang to life. She snuck a glance at him again. He was trying to look innocent, but she could tell from his dimples and the heat of his gaze that he had some idea of where her train of thought had derailed.

Returning her attention to her plate, Alisa speared a bit of steak and brought it to her mouth. As she chewed, she sensed his thoughtful gaze focused on her.

Uncertain what to say, she continued to eat, letting the silence grow. Under the table, Zach's leg brushed against hers. Feeling playful and in the mood for some sensual payback of her own, she pressed her leg against his and shifted, gliding her calf against the inside of his leg. She had the satisfaction of seeing his eyes widen before a small grin curved his lips.

He lifted a bit of potato to his mouth and slowly closed his lips over the bite. Alisa's pulse jumped. As he pulled the fork out of his mouth, his firm lips pressed against the metal and she got a mental image of those same lips wrapped around her nipple, pulling at the peak. Her nipples hardened in response, echoing their yearning for the fantasy to be made real.

Self-conscious, she pulled her leg back and dipped her head, finishing the last of her food. Zach had a few bites left, which was good because she was lightheaded with the need to kiss him. Despite the pleasure of watching him eat and making it seem wicked, she wanted to finally feel his naked flesh against hers.

After swallowing his last bite of salad, Zach glanced at her empty plate and pushed his aside. His blue eyes met hers and the flirty mood left Alisa. The heat in his eyes was overlaid by gentleness and she knew the time had come for some answers. He wasn't going to let it go without getting them. As he reached across the table to lay his hands over her suddenly clammy ones, she licked her dry lips.

"You ready for that talk?" The compassion in his voice as he spoke made her wonder if he already knew what she was going to say.

"Let's get some coffee and sit outside."

Wanting to break away for a moment to gather her thoughts and her words, she pulled away from him and stood, her chair scraping along the hardwood floor. Wincing at the sound, she hurried to the sink and reached to pull two cups off the rack. A hard warmth pressed against her back as Zach reached over her, easily grabbing the cups.

After he set them on the counter, his hands molded against her hips, holding her tight against him while she filled the cups with coffee. His lips pressed against her neck, treading soft kisses along the slender column until she squirmed away.

"Stop that," she scolded teasingly, not really minding. "I'm trying to pour hot coffee." Her stomach fluttered at the touch of his erection pressing against her back. She shifted her hips, just lightly gliding over his groin, just enough to earn her a swift inhalation.

Zach pressed another soft kiss, this time at the delicate curve where her shoulder and neck met, then grabbed his cup of coffee and led the way to her back porch. He settled his large frame in her rocker and put his cup on the table beside him, as if he hadn't a care in the world. She might have believed it too, if she didn't know him so well. As she went to sit in the chair beside him, he grabbed her hips and pulled her down into his lap.

Alisa froze for a moment as her adrenalin spiked, but when his hands let her go, she was able to relax against him. After placing her coffee beside his, she twisted to the side and snuggled against him, tucking her head under his chin. His arousal rubbed against her hip. In its own way, that too was familiar. He was turned on, and making no moves to change the situation. Curled up in his arms, she wanted to enjoy the moment, rather than rehashing the past. But it couldn't wait any longer--she had already waited so long to tell him. As she went to open her mouth, he spoke.

"Just answer me one question and if it's a yes, we'll let the matter go until you choose to talk about it." He paused, and she nodded.

"Were you raped?"

Every muscle in his body tightened as he waited for her response. Holding back her tears, she nodded against him, knowing he could feel the slight motion against his chest.

"Fuck!" Despite his harsh tone, Alisa knew he wasn't mad at her.

"I lied. I can't--There's no way--" he stumbled, unable to complete the thought. "Damn-it! Alisa, who was it? Do you know? I'm going to track the son of a--"

Leaning back against his arm, she pressed a finger against his lips. "Shhh. It was a long time ago, and tonight is so perfect. I don't want to ruin it." As crazy as it seemed, the night was perfect. The insects were cooperating and the night air had a slight nip to it, just enough to let her curl tighter against him for warmth.

"Damnit baby, I...why didn't you tell me? You shouldn't have had to go through that alone. I would have been there for you--"

Unwilling to waste a moment more, two years was already too much, Alisa pressed a quick kiss against his lips, halting his words.

"I can't--I won't--talk about this now. I don't want to tarnish what we have, right here and now. Please Zach, just kiss me."

His hand trembling, Zach cupped the back of her neck and pulled her into his kiss. Soft as a butterfly, his lips danced over hers, until Alisa was ready to scream her frustration. This was what she didn't want, his handling her with kid gloves. She would rather not have him at all than to have only a part of him. As much as she had kidded herself, it was his intensity she craved. The single-minded pursuit of what he wanted.

Deciding to take matters into her own hands, she pressed tighter against him and deepened the kiss. Zach held back at first, his hands lightly running up and down her back.

Growing bolder, Alisa danced her tongue along his. Breaking the kiss, she nipped at his lower lip with her teeth and then thrust her tongue back into his mouth. With a soft growl, Zach responded, his hands dropping to cup the soft curve of her ass.

Restless, Alisa shifted in his arms, so that she straddled him, her dress hiked halfway up her thighs. Pressing down against him, she felt his need, the hardness of his cock through his shorts. He didn't try to hide his reaction to her closeness and she thrilled at it. He wasn't afraid to let her know he was aroused. Her pussy fluttered, awakening for him.

His hands caressed up and down her thighs, slowly shifting her dress higher. Her skin prickled as the cool night air joined his hands in caressing her.

"Make love to me," she whispered against his lips.

"Are you sure?"

She had never been surer of anything in her life than she was in that moment. They were meant to be together, her body knew it. It was only her foolish pride and her fears that had kept them apart for so long. So much lost time.

"Yes, Zach, I'm sure."

DIGGIN UP BONES
Chapter Five

Alisa stood and straightened her dress, then held out her hand. Zach laid his hand in hers, and allowed her to lead him into the house. Just inside the door, he paused and pulled her into his embrace, holding her loosely against his chest. Zach leaned back against the door and she settled against him, trying to burrow into his warmth. With his knees slightly bent, Alisa was able to lean forward and kiss him without having to stretch.

Pouring all the love and desire she could into the kiss, she sought to convince him that this was what she wanted. She knew she succeeded when he cupped her ass and lifted her against him. She locked her legs around his waist, not letting him slide her down. Pulling away from the wall, he carried her wrapped around him. With each step he took, his erection rubbed against her, creating a delicious friction.

Between kisses, she guided him down the hall to her room. By the time he stepped across the threshold of her bedroom, she was ready to scream, she needed him so badly.

When he stopped in the middle of her room, Alisa unlocked her legs and slowly straightened, her breasts brushing along his chest. She delighted at the deep rumble of his groan. Reflexively, his hands grasped her hips, holding her tight against him as his head swooped down and he kissed her. Twining her arms around his neck, she clung to him, letting him dominate their embrace. His hands shifted against her, restlessly moving over her back and hips as he pressed into the cradle of her body, his cock hard and straining between them. Lightheaded, she broke the kiss.

Stepping back, she moved into a shaft of moonlight and slid the straps of her dress from her shoulders. Zach's gaze followed her every movement. Knowing that if she hesitated she might lose her nerve, she gathered her courage and let her dress flitter to the floor. His eyes darkened from their unearthly pale blue to wet blue velvet.

A thrill of feminine awareness rushed through her. Inexperienced at sex, she was still getting him turned on. Then again, she'd always been able to do that. Many of their dates had ended with a kiss and some heavy petting, where she could feel the weight of his erection pressing against her. But then, like now, he waited--letting her set the pace.

Unclasping her bra, she tossed it aside, then shimmed out of her panties before she could change her mind. She turned her back to him and moved to the bed, where she darted a quick glance at him over her shoulder before laying down. The sheets felt cool against her skin, heightening her awareness of her body. Knowing he wouldn't take it for granted, she held her arms out, inviting him into her embrace.

With a groan that sounded like he was being tortured, Zach climbed onto the bed and pressed against her, rolling them both to lie on their sides, facing each other. His work-calloused hands brushed against the smoothness of her skin, sending shivers down her spine. Gently, as if he was afraid she'd shatter, he ran his hands up and down her body, gliding over her hips and ass, then working their way back up to her neck, before starting all over again.

Restlessly, she shifted against him, grinding her body against his. Her nipples ached for his caress. Every beat of her heart throbbed in her clit. Needing to be touched, she slid her hands down her body, pressing them between her thighs to caress her tender flesh.

His eyes smoky, Zach leaned back to watch her, his hands continuing to caress her with soft touches, cupping and loving her breasts before siding down to her hips.

"God, baby, you feel so good," he whispered, approval in his voice as she slipped a finger past her lips and into her aching depths. Hesitantly, he slid a hand down her body and thrust his finger to join hers. Alisa purred as she arched into his touch, driving both their fingers deeper.

His teeth nipped at her breasts, and then his tongue lapped away the hurt. "You like that?"

"Yes," she hissed, thrusting another finger deep. Her pussy clenched around them, but it wasn't enough. Looking into his eyes, she saw his intention moments before he dipped his head and pressed soft kisses against her stomach, dipping his tongue into the valley of her belly button. He pulled his finger out of her, and Alisa picked up the speed of her own thrusts, plunging her two fingers into her core. She whimpered at the texture of his tongue rasping over her skin as he moved slowly downward, lapping at her pubic bone before settling between her thighs.

The material of his shirt brushed against her inner thighs as he shifted, his breath rushing over her heated flesh. And then his tongue was there, licking her fingers as she pulled them out, and then sliding in with them. Arching her back, she tried to get closer, to draw his tongue deeper within her. But Zach pulled back and pressed soft kisses against her inner thighs.

Alisa undulated on the bed, trying to get closer, her body knowing what it wanted even if she couldn't put it to words to ask for it. With the heat of Zach's gaze on her, she looked down the sleek lines of her body and saw half of his face visible over her mound. His eyes--so light and eerily blue--sparkled with an inner flame.

As his teeth nipped at her skin, Alisa arched upwards. It was too much. She wanted him against her when she climaxed. Unlike her fantasies, he was real, and his cock was just a plea away from thrusting into her, filling her in the way she had craved for so long.

"Please, Zach," she cried, her body trembling in need. "Let me feel you against me."

With one last flick of his tongue against her thigh, he sat up. Her body mourned the loss of his when he slid off the bed. His gaze locked on her as he slowly eased his shirt off, tossing it aside. Alisa let her eyes trail over him, admiring the way he'd grown into his frame. He had a lot of muscle mass he didn't before and yet his chest was still devoid of hair. Her fingers itched to slide over him, learning all the places he liked to be touched.

When his hands went to the waistband of his shorts, her mouth went dry. This was the point of no return. One flinch from her, one sign of distress or hesitation, and he'd stop. She didn't know if she would survive if he did.

He slid his shorts and underwear down and stepped out of them. Her breath caught as she viewed his length for the first time. Hard and flushed, it was a little intimidating, but breathtaking nonetheless. She had to experience him sliding into her, marking her with his passion. The anticipation was killing her.

She continued playing with her pussy with her hand and started stroking up and down her stomach with the other. "There are condoms in the nightstand."

"That sure of me?" Despite his attempt to lighten the moment, she could hear the undercurrent of worry in his voice.

Trying to dispel it, she shook her head and responded with a grin, "That hopeful."

Zach's eyes sparkled in the dim light as he pressed the condom against the tip of his cock and started to unroll it over his length. His movements transfixed Alisa. She watched as he stroked his hand up and down his cock, pressing the latex against his skin. Soon, that thin layer of latex would be all that separated them.

As he carefully climbed on the bed and pressed against her, she reached for him. She stroked his cock with inexperienced hands. The texture of the Latex was a curious sensation, but she could feel the heat of his skin beneath it. His hips bucked when she rolled her thumb over his cock-head so she did it again.

"Damn, baby, you make me quiver."

Slipping her fingers from her pussy, she pressed her hand against his chest and tenderly pushed. He rolled onto his back; she sat up and threw a leg over his waist. Straddling him, she eased herself onto his cock, guiding him into her. As the first inch pressed in, she drew in a deep breath. Looking into his eyes, she sank down another inch. She felt her body stretching to accommodate him. Trying to relax her muscles, even as she worried it would hurt, she lowered herself another inch.

Zach groaned softly, his hands caressing his thighs. His touch exhilarated her. She was taking control of her life. She was intimately joined with the only man she had ever loved, and she was obviously turning him on.

She'd been using a battery-operated boyfriend for a while now, but it didn't compare to the real thing in length or girth. The heat and curve of his cock added a dimension plastic never could. Sucking in another deep breath, she held it and ground down

38

against him. Alisa thought she'd pass out as he seemed to fill her completely, his cock pressing against all of her slick inner walls so deliciously.

Zach's hands fisted in the bed sheet as she slowly rocked back and forth on him. Beads of sweat broke out on his forehead as he restrained himself. Her heart bursting with love for him, she tightened her pussy around his cock.

He raised his hands to her breasts, his thumb rolling over her rock hard nipples. Looking down, the sight of his tanned fingers pinching and tweaking her coral colored nipples on her otherwise fair skin caused her pussy to clench in pleasure.

"I need more," she whimpered, jerking against him. "I don't know...I feel so...please, Zach."

His eyes watchful, he moved beneath her. Alisa gasped at the sensations caused by just the slight movement of his cock within her. Closing her eyes, she tossed her head back and gave herself up to the bliss--trusting Zach completely to keep her safe.

A cascade of sensations rushed through her. Deep within her stomach, a curious tightness started. She had experienced a similar sensation each time she masturbated, but this was different--more intense. Almost scared, she squeezed her body around Zach's.

His grip, rough with passion, cupped the back of her neck and pulled her down to his lips. His tongue swept past her lips, laying claim to all that she was, and would ever be. In that moment, she felt whole for the first time in years.

Moaning into his mouth, she coaxed him on without words. He seemed to understand before she did, knew what would give her the most pleasure, as his hands brushed over her body, igniting tiny fires of desire. The tightness expanded until she was sure it was going to swallow her. Then, in a rush, it collapsed, taking her with it.

She threw back her head and screamed faintly as her world exploded. Her pussy tightened around his cock, milking him, silently begging him to join her in that perfect moment. His breath harsh against her ear, he answered her wish as his hips jerked against her.

Collapsing against him, struggling to control her breathing, Alisa pressed Zach against the bed. By the sound of him, he was having just as much trouble recovering.

"My God," she gasped.

"Mmm."

Her eyes heavy with the need to sleep, Alisa moaned in protest when Zach pulled out of her arms and got out of bed. "I have to flush the condom," he explained, motioning at his now soft cock.

"Hurry back," she whispered.

He returned moments later, his skin still glowing with a light sheen of sweat. Rather than climb into bed with her, he leaned down and lifted her into his arms. Her body sated and deliciously worn out, Alisa managed only a token protest as Zach carried her into the bathroom. He had already started the water, and the steam was warming the room.

Rather than set her down beside the tub, Zach stepped into it, holding her in his arms. As her feet touched the cool tile, Zach wrapped an arm around her waist and held her pressed against him while he grabbed the soap.

"I know you're tired, baby, but you'll feel a lot better in the morning if we take a quick shower."

Alisa shifted until she was standing in front of him, her back pressed against his chest, and closed her eyes. His hands free, Zach made quick work of soaping her front, only pausing occasionally to sooth and stroke her stomach and sides, then down along the outsides of her legs. Her breasts and mound were efficiently washed with the lightest of touches.

Turning, Alisa burrowed against his chest, inhaling the masculine scent of him as he soaped her back and then washed his hands off.

"Just a few moments more."

The sensation of his hands running through her hair, washing the sweat from the red strands, had Alisa trembling by the time he washed her hair out. She was a mass of pampered flesh by the time he was done, content to let him wash her hair over and over, until she ran out of shampoo.

Leaving the water still running, he picked her up again, grabbed a towel as he passed by the rack, and carried her back to her bedroom. Lovingly, he dried every inch of her, then tucked her in bed. Alisa's eyes fluttered open at the sound of moving him away.

"Don't go..." she whispered, so soft she didn't even know if she spoke aloud.

"I'll be right back, baby. I need to finish up."

A few minutes later, the bed dipped as Zach climbed in, still damp from his shower, and settled himself next to her. Alisa rolled over, climbing half on top of him. Her leg thrown over his waist, she cuddled against him, her head pressed against his heart. Listening to the steady thump, thump, she drifted off to sleep, safe in his arms.

DIGGIN UP BONES
Chapter Six

Alisa woke to the sound of people moving around in her backyard. Glaring at the open window, she tried to pull a pillow over her head, but it was stuck under something. Rolling over, she looked right into Zach's sleepy blue gaze.

"Morning," he drawled, his voice thick with sleep.

She whispered back, "Good morning."

Never having had a morning after before, she was uncertain what to do. One thing she did know, the sheet she'd kicked around her ankles in her sleep needed to be up and over her body. One of his crew could walk past the window at any time. She shifted on the bed, trying subtly to cover herself.

"Regrets?"

Despite the softness of his voice, Alisa heard the worry. The possibility of being seen didn't matter any more, comforting and reassuring him did. Kicking the sheet back down to the foot of the bed, she wrapped herself around him, cuddling against his strong body. "Nope, not a one. You?"

Now she was the one who waited with held breath. His crew had to have seen his truck already and wondered where he was.

"None." Tenderly his hands stroked her back and shoulders, brushing her skin so softly she almost couldn't feel his touch. "But I should get out there and referee the children."

Alisa shifted her head on his chest, her arms holding tight to him. "Don't go yet."

She was uncertain how to act, what to say. But lying in his arms felt so natural, she knew she didn't want to give that up. His hands gripped her arm, gently squeezing, before he sighed. "You're going to be sore, baby, and as much as I want to stay here with

42

you, I'm worried that if I do, we will get carried away and turn soreness into pain."

Alisa shivered just thinking about it, his cock hard and deep within her. Sliding her hand down his chest, she glided lower until she grasped his hardness, and started leisurely stroking him.

Curious to see what he would let her get away with, she pressed a soft kiss against his chest and started kissing a trail down to his stomach, and still further down. She turned around in the bed, so that she knelt facing his feet. She knew she was teasing him, with his lower body within easy reach, and her breasts almost resting on his fingertips. Zach inhaled sharply, but let her play until she reached his belly button.

"Alisa, sweetheart, you don't know what you're doing to me," he groaned out, his voice tight as she shifted her position and dragged her tongue across his cock-head. Swirling her tongue over the tip, she savored her first taste of his salty skin.

As his hands reached for her, she shifted sideways, giving his questing fingers access to her body. One hand played with her hair, sliding the red tresses between his fingers, while his other hand stroked along her breasts and side.

Wrapping her lips around his erection, she sucked him a couple of inches into her mouth. Zach's hips jerked and he groaned. Encouraged, she pulled back and stroked her tongue along the underside of his length. At his groan, she wrapped her lips around him again and worked up and down, taking him more fully into her mouth with each downward slide, just like she had with her pussy the night before. Just remembering it caused her inner muscles to contract.

His fingers found their goal and stroked along her lips before one dipped into her core, stroking along her slick inner walls. Whimpering softly, Alisa ground down against them as she continued her exploration of his erection. With gentle motions, Zach slid another finger in, and spread them apart within her. She could feel her body adjusting, widening to welcome his touch.

Cupping his balls in her hand, she gently squeezed them, causing them to roll and shift slightly in her grasp. Zach's hand jerked, driving his fingers deeper. With a moan, Alisa arched closer and pumped her hips. As his thumb rolled over her clit, and his fingers pumped in and out of her pussy, Alisa's orgasm built.

Given the steady flow of Zach's pre-come in her mouth, and the way his body tightened against her, she believed he was about there, too.

Tightening her lips around his cock, she slid down as far as she could and sucked hard, determined that he join her. She rocked gently on Zach's hand as he slid a third finger into her core and curled them, mimicking the girth of his cock. Wildly, she undulated, manipulating her body into an orgasm.

His hand fisted in her hair tighter and he groaned, pushing her away. His cock slid free with a muted pop, and she dropped her head against his hip. As she rode the waves of her orgasm, the molten heat of his come painted her hand as she still cupped his balls.

Breathless, she lay still, waiting for her heart to stop pounding. Despite Zach's labored breathing, his hands moved tirelessly over her body, rubbing soothing circles on her back and stroking her hair.

As subtly as she could, she raised her hand to her lips and tentatively licked at the back of her hand. Wrinkling her nose, she debated if she liked the taste, even as she wiped her hand against the sheets.

As her eyelids fluttered open, she lifted her head and shifted to lie against Zach, and pillowed her head on his chest again.

"I love you," he whispered, his voice tentative.

Lightheaded, she whispered back, "I know. I love you too."

After pressing a kiss against the top of her head, Zach spoke again, his voice tinged with regret. "And as much as I would love to stay here all day and cuddle with you, I am now definitely in need of another shower. Besides, the crew is going to need me soon."

As if on cue, a loud voice hollered out for a hand-shovel. Burrowing her face against his chest, Alisa struggled to hold on to the moment just a few seconds longer. As another voice bellowed a response, she sighed and sat up.

"Will you stay for dinner tonight, too?" she asked, trying to sound nonchalant and failing miserably.

Zach pressed a kiss against her neck, his whiskers tickling her like they always used to. "Definitely." He pressed another kiss. "And the night after that."

Alisa leaned back, and let the next kiss fall on her lips.

"And the night after that," he whispered against her lips, before sweeping his tongue past them into a deep kiss, then pulled back to continue, "And every night after that."

DIGGIN UP BONES
Chapter Seven

A few months later

A knock on the front door pulled Alisa from her writing. Saving her progress, she stood and pushed her chair under her desk, then headed down the hall. At the door, she paused and called out "Who's there?"

"Mail delivery, ma'am."

Giving a small groan, she opened the door and signed for her package. Glancing at the sender, she sighed. It was the galley of her manuscript. As happy as she was that it was one step closer to being published, it also meant a delay in her current manuscript. And she was on a roll with it.

"Thank you." After handing back the tablet, she tossed the package on the hall table.

"Thank you, ma'am."

Closing the door behind the delivery man, she turned and headed back down the hall to her office. A flicker of movement from outside caught her attention, and rather than return to her writing, she leaned against the window frame and watched Zach move around the yard, wrapping up the dig. The representative from the Cherokee Nation had been on site for more than five months, helping Zach preserve the artifacts.

Now it was ending and the team was moving on to a new site now that Zach had helped secure the funding. Things were returning to normal. Her yard, however, would never be the same again. Thanks to the dig team turning up the soil, and Zach helping with the plantings, she had the vegetable garden she had initially planned on. In addition, there was also an herb garden, a few small flowerbeds, and most of a walkway to the new barn she was having built for Ares. But they'd discovered six sets of remains that were being moved to proper burial grounds and untold amounts of information about the Cherokee who had once roamed the area, so she considered the disruptions well worth it. The professor in charge of the Archeology Department had even agreed to let her write the foreword to the paper he and Zach were working up about the dig.

As the light caught on the diamond of her ring, Alisa's heart tightened. She would never be the same again either. Admiring the way the diamond glinted in the sunlight, she gave a contented sigh. A few months ago, she had dreaded every moment she spent with Zach, and now she couldn't get enough time with him.

Thankfully, he had opted out of leading the next dig and was taking a vacation to help her with her research, while working on his thesis for his Master's degree. A small smile creased the corners of her mouth as she remembered how Zach had helped her the evening before. They had been elbows deep in stacks of old, dusty records, when he had turned to her with a twinkle in his eyes and suggested a more pleasurable pastime.

Playfully, she had pouted and he set about convincing her to his point of view. They had ended up in front of the mirror in their bedroom, and while she had watched their reflection, he had run his hands over her body, touching and caressing her until she was begging him to make love to her.

Then he had dropped to his knees before her and, with her hands fisted in his hair, she watched as he tongued her to orgasm. After she could breathe again, she had enjoyed turning the tables, and had made him stand still and watch as she had brought him to his own orgasm.

That particular bit of research wasn't going into the book.

Pressing her palm against the glass, she savored the sight of her fiancée's long legged stride eating up the distance as he touched base with each member of the clean up crew and wrapped everything up.

As if aware of her attention, Zach turned and cupped a hand over his eyebrows, shielding his eyes as he met her gaze through her window. His tanned skin glistened with a light sheen of sweat, and the top buttons of his shirt had slid undone with his movements.

Her heart skipped a beat as she looked down at him, counting the hours until he would be done and they would be able to be together. She gave a shiver just thinking about it, and from the grin Zach flashed at her, he was thinking something along the same lines.

After glancing at her ring once more, she returned to her writing, smiling at the knowledge that in just a few weeks she would be Mrs. Alisa Bradford, part time writer, full time satisfied woman.

Want just a little bit more of Alisa and Zach?
Keep reading for their first Christmas together ...

DIGGIN UP BONES: WRITING OF LOVE

Alisa hands trembled as she watched Zach peel back the edge of the wrapping paper on his present. Sitting across from her, he laughed softly at her anxious expression. With it being their first Christmas together, she wasn't sure what to expect. Married only a few months, everything was still new and a learning experience.

Unable to go on an extended honeymoon due to Zach's graduate work, they had opted to stay at her house and lock themselves in for a few days. The week before the wedding was hectic as some of his workers from the dig helped move his things into her house. Now the home was a blend of both of them, perfectly meshed together. Except for her study--that was the one room Zach left all hers. As a full-time writer, she needed a sanctuary to retreat to when her characters demanded her attention.

As his sun-browned hands folded back the paper she had painstakingly wrapped around the bound advanced review copy she held her breath as her gift was revealed.

Zach's blue-eyed gaze traced over the elaborate lettering of the title: *Resurrecting Memories of Love*. Alisa nervously plucked at the tie of her robe, waiting for his reaction.

"You wrote this for me?" he asked, his voice rough with emotion. Alisa nodded, her own throat tight. She had worked on the project in between deadlines, determined to see it come to fruition, even if she really didn't have time to write it. It was their story--the tale of a man whose feelings were so great he was willing to see beyond the walls the emotionally damaged heroine had put up, to the love they could have together. With patience, he showed her a world she had only dreamt of, but wasn't brave enough to reach for on her own. Different from anything else she had even written, it dripped with innocence and passion, and echoed her feelings for Zach.

"Damn baby, thank you," he whispered, tears welling in his eyes.

Her agent loved it, but the only opinion that mattered to her was Zach's. Leaning back against the couch, his long legs stretched out on the floor toward her, he flipped the cover open and began reading. Alisa climbed to her feet and left the room, leaving him with his gift.

Several hours later, Zach wrapped his strong arms around her waist as she washed the dishes. His whole dig team, people they now considered their extended family after all they had been through together, had come over to share Christmas Eve dinner with them, and it had been a full house.

His warm lips pressed soft kisses along the curve of her neck as he pulled the lapels of her robe apart and bared flesh to his touch. Still tingling from the loving making that had heralded in their first Christmas morning, her nerves quickly flared to life. Need hummed throughout her body, rekindled so easily by his touch. Like magic, his fingers played her with clit until she was a quivering mass of sensation. Coaxing her backwards, he sat down in a chair at the kitchen table and pulled her into his lap, his long fingers gliding over her flesh as he brought her to an earth-shattering climax, her cries ringing through the stillness of the room.

"Every time I think my heart will burst with love for you, you manage to fill it just a little bit more. I love the book, and I love that you wrote it for me."

Alisa blushed as he turned her in his lap and kissed her, his cock hard and pressing against her thigh. Wrapping her arms around his neck, she embraced the passion arcing between them, something that, just a few months before, would have terrified her. Her love welling in her chest, Alisa gave Zach one more Christmas gift--her unrestrained passion; without fear, without hesitation.

A BID FOR LOVE

Erika couldn't take her eyes off the painting. The imagery was intoxicating. The way the shadows folded over the couple entwined in the bed, the leaves along the edge of the window that hinted at a forbidden tryst. The way the vines crept over the glass in strategic places kept it from being tawdry and gave it a dreamy quality.

She had been trying for almost two years to track down all of her grandmother's work, and finally she was about to bid on the last piece—what was probably the best work she had ever done. Her uncle, may he rot in Hell, had sold off the family legacy to pay his gambling debts. She and her mother had been doing all they could to find the paintings and purchase them. Some had slipped through their fingers, held in a private collection, but a few months ago they had come back into the market with the owner's death.

This last painting, created for a former lover of her grandmother's almost fifty years before, was being sold at auction by his estate. She had been hesitant to approach the aging gentleman about purchasing the painting, since it was one of the few that had been given, not sold away. All the others given away had been returned to her grandmother or her family upon the owner's death, save this one.

It was frustrating waiting on the bidding for the last piece to be auctioned off before her grandmother's painting was up on the block. Although most of the works being sold weren't by a well known artist, the quality of them was evident. Finally, the auctioneer banged his gavel and issued the final declaration "Sold!"

Flicking her gaze around the room, she tried to gauge who was interested in the next painting when the sight of a familiar gray suit caught her attention. Looking up the owner's body, her gaze met laughing blue eyes, lips curled in a mocking smile. Ryan Carstairs.

"This next painting is by Virginia Gleeson, a local artist, somewhat renowned as being an eccentric lady. She was married young, widowed after only three years, and chose to remain alone, while raising her two young children. She loved life, which is evident in the vibrancy of her works. She also had a passionate nature, which is captured by her subject material. Almost all of her later works are of couples forever locked in each other's embrace."

Erika knew the material of her grandmother's paintings quite well; she owned one of the very last paintings she'd completed. Her grandmother had surprised her with it on her birthday. Unfortunately, she was no longer with the man in it, and it only served to bring back bad memories of a time she would rather forget.

But she held on to it, and it held a place of honor on her wall, with a black sheet carefully draped over it. She hoped one day to be able to look at it without feeling her heart breaking for what had been.

"For this painting, we'll start the bidding at five hundred. Do I have five hundred?"

Erika waited a moment to see how the bidding would progress. She didn't want to jump in too early and start a bidding war with anyone, but after five bids, when the price reached seven-fifty Ryan jumped in, bumping it to a thousand.

Heart heavy, she looked at him and raised her paddle as the auctioneer asked if anyone would go eleven hundred. At that point the last holdout dropped out, and Erika waited, hoping Ryan would just let it go. There was no way he didn't know he was bidding on her grandmother's painting; he had helped her track down a few of the missing works. She suspected that was precisely why he was there, because of her grandmother's painting.

She recalled how quickly love had turned into something else, removing all affection and leaving only painful memories. Once they had been so in love they couldn't stand to be apart for more than a few hours. Now, he was raising his paddle with a derisive twist to his lips and a nod in her direction.

Meeting the challenge in his gaze, she raised the bid again.

As the price climbed, Erika felt her nerves stretch tight. Ryan had always had that effect on her, but not normally so unpleasantly. Anticipation of his return home from work would always leave her with damp palms, her breath coming just a little bit quicker. It was accentuated often by what she was wearing as she waited on him. Normally it was simple lingerie, or a leather bustier. But sometimes he would ask her to lie on the bed wearing a mask, her body completely nude, her limbs resting in the valley of padded cuffs, waiting for him to close them around her wrists and ankles.

Those were the days she longed for the most, the innocent seduction of submitting to his dominating ways, of feeling him stroke her body with a soft whip before the whistle of it sung through the air, and the crack of it landed against her tender skin.

It had been perfect.

When her grandmother had gifted her with the painting of the two of them laying together on a white canvas, no sheets or other decorations to detract from the passion of their embrace, she hadn't had the heart to let the aging woman know a key item was missing, specifically a collar around her neck.

Shaking her head at herself, Erika returned her gaze to the auctioneer as she countered Ryan's latest bid, taking the cost to eighteen-fifty. Knowing she could only go a few hundred higher tortured her. She was so close, but as the bids continued, and the price jumped to twenty-one hundred, she had to admit defeat. The auctioneer asked for twenty-two hundred, asked again, then looked at her and asked for twenty-one fifty. Raising her paddle, Erika accepted the bid, then held her breath as the bid was asked again for twenty-two hundred.

"We have twenty-two hundred from the gentleman in the back. Do I have twenty-three hundred? Anyone? Twenty-three hundred for this breathtaking Virginia Gleeson painting? No? twenty-two fifty? Anyone? Then sold for twenty-two hundred to the gentleman in the back. If you'll come up front, please.

"Our next painting ..."

Erika tuned out the auctioneer as he started in about the details of the next artwork. Gathering her purse and folder, she stood and walked to the back of the room. A warm hand wrapped around her elbow and jerked her to a halt.

"We need to talk."

Looking into Ryan's gaze, Erika felt her heart tighten. She wanted to scream at him for buying her grandmother's painting, but the memory of how much she used to love him held her silent.

Bitterness swirled around her as she pulled away from him and opened the doors.

"If you want a chance at that painting, you'll hear me out."

Erika almost didn't stop, but knowing how heart broken her mother would be if she ever found out there was a last chance to get the painting back, forced her to stop. Her mother had taken the loss of her own mother just a few months earlier very hard. It had renewed her determination that they find and acquire all of her paintings.

"Meet me in the hallway in five minutes."

Nodding her head without looking back, Erika stepped into the opening between the heavy oak doors and allowed them to swing closed behind her. Pressing a palm against her chest, she could feel her heart racing. She managed to drop into one of the antique chairs that lined the hallway, her mind whirling with thoughts about what Ryan could want.

Devastatingly handsome, born into a wealthy family, Ryan still had a down-to-earth quality about him. Part of that was thanks to his father's determination that his son not grow up thinking the world owed him anything. Ryan had once confessed, their bodies still glistening with sweat and the juices of their shared passion, that he owed his old man for that. He appreciated everything he had.

Unfortunately, a few months later, Erika knew it had all been a lie. He hadn't appreciated her. Clenching her fingers, she could still feel the coldness wash over her body as she had held the newspaper article announcing Ryan's upcoming marriage to a socialite friend of the family. He had always laughed off their appearing together in public as her being a friend of the family.

He'd shrug and respond, "Her family and mine have been close friends for generations." Swearing she had nothing to worry about, he would inevitably seduce her into not thinking about anything anymore, except him.

But that day everything had changed. He had come to his house to find her packing. Anger had flared in his eyes as he watched her throwing her clothing into a pile in her suitcase. "You're not even going to give me a chance to explain?"

Erika closed her eyes as she remembered the pain that had threaded through her at his hurt tone. She was the one who had been injured, lied to, betrayed, strung along with pretty words and declarations of love, until she had bought into the fantasy that maybe they could have a life together. Unable to deal with the emotions overwhelming her, she had choked on her answer and settled for shaking her head as she slammed the lid closed.

As she forced the zipper to slide around the bulging case, his hands had grabbed her arms and spun her around. Before she could gain her balance he had gripped her forearms and pulled her against him, his lips smacking down on hers in a kiss unlike any he had ever pressed against her. He was like a man possessed as he demanded entrance into her mouth. Licking her lips, she had the phantom sensation that she could still taste her tears melded with the taste of his lips.

As suddenly as he had grabbed her, Ryan thrust her away from himself, and stabbed a hand into his hair. Shaken to the core, she had turned and grabbed her case, her heart screaming at him to try to explain, to demand she hear him out. Instead he opened the bedroom door and held it for her. "Go on then, get the hell out," he spit out, his light eyes flashing angrily at her.

Holding the case against her side, Erika had walked out as proudly as she could manage, blinded by her own tears.

"I see you waited on me." Drawn back to the present by his mocking words, Erika stood up and faced him head on.

"Why did you buy that painting? You could have had anything else in the auction, or in any other auction. Why that painting?"

Ryan took a step closer to her, and Erika could feel the heat coming off his body. Despite his business suit and his high-class haircut, she could feel the baser animal in him just beneath the surface.

It was what first attracted her to him, that barely leashed intensity, covered by a thin layer of gentility.

"How badly do you want the painting?"

Erika ground her teeth at his ignoring her question, but wasn't about to give him the satisfaction of repeating herself. Nor was she going to answer him. She wasn't about to hint at her desperation.

Her mother had promised her grandmother on her deathbed that she would track down all the rest of her paintings and keep them in the family, using the insurance money to foot the bill. While not wealthy in life, she had had the sense to get a sizable policy on herself early on, wanting to make sure her children were provided for if she passed on while they were younger. Habit had kept her paying the premiums.

The knowledge that her own son had sold her prized possessions had eaten at her in the last few months, destroying what was left of her once robust health. And now, with her own mother having taken a turn for the worse, Erika was determined she would have all of her grandmother's works around her, if it was the last thing she did. She wasn't about to let Ryan Carstairs stand in her way.

Putting her hands on her hips, she looked him right in the eyes and asked, "What are you asking for it?"

She knew whatever it was, she wasn't going to like it. Not judging by the smile on his lips. "I'll give it to you, free and clear— a gift."

Erika waited, knowing he wasn't done yet. Ryan was too shrewd a business man to just fork over two grand without some kind of condition.

"After you spend forty-eight hours with me."

Erika raised her gaze to his eyes, wanting to judge the seriousness of his words. Forty-eight hours in his company would seem a lifetime, but it might finally exercise him from her life once and for all.

"There are a few conditions however. First, it will be at my place. Second, you agree to submit to me completely for those forty-eight hours, at the end of which, you are free to walk away with the painting."

Erika could feel her eyes widening. If he actually expected what she thought he expected, he was out of his mind. After almost a year, he expected to drop back into her life and her bed, without a moment's pause? She knew his engagement had fallen through for him, but that didn't mean she wanted him back in her life.

Mentally stomping on the flickering desire to feel his touch again that ignited in the back of her mind, she shook her head, wanting to scream at him that she wasn't his plaything anymore.

But she couldn't. She had to do whatever she could to get the painting back, and two days as his sex slave wasn't anything she hadn't done before. She had spent an entire week at his place once, dressed in a gauzy gown that hid nothing. He had loved bending her over the furniture and slowly taking her from behind, lifting her onto the table and feasting on her pussy until she cried with the need to orgasm. His fingers had spent more time buried between her pussy lips, or his cock in her mouth, than any other man. It was a week in paradise, and one of her fondest memories of him.

Looking up at him, she could see the wheels turning in his mind. He knew, damn him. "Any other conditions?" She forced herself to sound calm.

His nostrils flared. Erika could see the pulse throbbing at the base of his neck. He knew he had her, now all he had to do was seal the deal.

"Yes, one more. You don't talk, unless I give you permission, but you have to listen to everything I say, every last word."

Feeling like she was about to step into the vortex of a tornado, Erika held out her hand for Ryan to shake. As his larger one clasped hers, the heat of his touch sent shivers of sexual awareness down her spine. Possessively he closed his fingers around hers.

Pulling her even closer, he leaned down and whispered a breath away from her lips, "I'll send a driver for you on Friday at eight. Don't pack anything except for personal hygiene products."

Erika pulled away before she could do something stupid like close the nanometer separating them and kiss him. Finding strength somewhere inside she hadn't known before, she walked away from him, and didn't look back.

* * *

Unfortunately, by Friday she had lost all the emotional strength she had gained and was a jumbled mess inside. At the time, surviving forty-eight hours with Ryan hadn't seemed like such a big deal, but now, with it nearing, she was anything but certain. He really was everything she wanted in a guy, with one exception—he was a cheating, lying, using bastard.

But just the sound of his voice could make her cream her panties, let alone the touch of his hand against her skin, pushing her to the bed and claiming her body, letting her know he was in charge.

When they were out together, when they were relaxing, or just hanging out, he had always treated her like an equal, despite their economic differences. However, when it came to anything sexual, he was in charge and they both knew it.

She couldn't count the number of times she had looked at the painting of the two of them, staring at the look of joy on her face as she gazed up at him, so perfectly rendered by her grandmother's hand and imagination. While there was an oddness to knowing the beloved woman had imagined her and her lover together, it was something she had grown up around. Her grandmother saw beauty in love and its physical expression, and it was her strength and her sheer passion that had allowed Erika to so readily accept submitting to Ryan, to letting him dominate her.

Her hands shaking, she fought the urge to take another look at the painting, to torture herself with the innocence she used to have where Ryan was concerned. She wanted to call the whole thing off, wanted to deny him further power over her.

It was too late to back out however. She had already told her mother the painting, the last of the ones done for former lovers, was being delivered on Monday. Glancing out the window she saw a black limo pull up. The door opened and a driver stepped out, the lines of his uniform crisp and perfect. Erika had a feeling Ryan planned a driver knowing she wouldn't pitch a fit with a stranger. He probably figured that by the time she got to his house she would be resigned to her fate of a weekend spent as his sex slave. Even if she wasn't, by not being allowed to talk, she wouldn't be able to vent her frustration.

At the polite knock, Erika took a deep breath, grabbed her overnight bag, and opened the door. The ride was relatively short, although it could have been two hours for all she knew. Dreading the forty-eight hours to come, the respite before the storm would never be long enough. By the time the limo pulled into the circular drive in front of Ryan's house however, she had managed to calm her nerves.

It wasn't that she would mind the sex. He had never let her down in that regard, never used her as means to his own relief without considering hers. If she could separate the emotions, a booty call from his talented cock was just what she needed. It was the fear of falling for him again, of the intense craving he generated inside of her, until he became a drug she was addicted to, that made her leery of his intentions.

About a month after she had walked out, news of the cancellation of his engagement came out. A few days later, a letter arrived in the mail for her. After glancing at near perfect handwriting, and lack of return address, she had shoved it into a box in the back of her closet alongside all the gifts he had give her. Despite her aching heart, she couldn't bear to throw away the notes he had written her, the pair of earrings he bought for her twenty-fifth birthday, the jewel collar with her name engraved on it and the other things he had given her over their time together.

The blast of cool air as the driver opened the door brought her back to the present, and without needing to be prodded, she climbed out of the plush interior and met Ryan head on. He was standing there waiting, and a rush of arousal washed over her body.

He was just as gorgeous as ever. Nose slightly crooked from a fight his junior year of high school, long legs encased in well-worn jeans, light eyes filled with laughter to a joke only he knew the punch line to, broad shoulders, and chest covered with the thin layer of a designer silk shirt.

Hating herself for responding to him so quickly, she allowed him to cup her elbow and guide her into the house. As the door closed behind her, he spun her around and let her go. Standing just inside the door was a crate, the name of the auction house across it in bold lettering. Ryan followed the direction of her gaze.

"In forty-eight hours, you can walk out of here with it. It will be sitting right there until then. If you don't trust me, I will show you the painting."

Erika shook her head, "No, I trust you." She could have bitten her tongue the moment the words were out of her mouth.

Ryan cocked a sardonic eyebrow at her, a humorless smile curling his lips. "If only that were true, but we both know it's not."

Ryan moved away from her, heading into the living room. Feeling off balance, Erika followed him, uncertain what he had in store for her. As she entered the dark room, a spark of light flickered off to her side. Ryan quickly lit the candle and blew out the match. Using the long tapered candle, he moved around the room lighting the others.

"Strip," he ordered as he moved about the room, his back still to her. Shrugging off her coat, Erika slowly pealed her T-shirt over her head and kicked off her sandals. Ryan finished his task and turned back around as she was sliding her jeans down her legs, baring her smoothly shaven pussy to the hunger of his gaze.

He eyed her like a starving man staring at a T-bone steak. Suddenly self-conscious, she gathered her clothing and neatly folded it, needing some task to take her focus away from his stare. As she set her shoes on top, Ryan reached out and pulled the stack from her hand. "You won't need these for a while."

Erika closed her eyes as he moved away with her clothing. Naked, she wouldn't be able to hide her body's reaction to him. Nor would she be able to gather the sense of shielding the clothing would offer. She was bare to him, in every sense of the word, and Ryan knew it.

It was how he often had asked her to be. She would spend entire weekends not wearing a stitch of clothing as she moved around the house doing simple chores, or simply relaxing with him and watching TV. Other times, he had expressed no orders one way or another, and she would spend hours deciding just what to wear, what would please him the most.

Shivering at the rekindled fires of her need to feel his fingers stroking over her body, she forced herself to remember the pain of finding out he was engaged. That he had lied to her, and had been seeing someone else, using her as a "fling" on the side. She often tortured herself, wondering if he had planned on asking her to be his mistress. She could understand the pressure of old wealth wanting to plan their children's nuptials. What kept her awake some nights wondering was if a loveless marriage was what his future held and she had known ahead of time, would she have agreed to such an arrangement? Would she have set aside her pride, and taken the scraps he could offer her, just to be with him?

"Are you hungry?"

Erika jumped as his voice sounded right behind her. She spun around to find him leaning against the doorway leading between the dining room and the living room, watching her. Somewhere along the way to wherever he had taken her clothing, he had removed his shirt and shoes, leaving him wearing only the jeans. Glancing down, she noticed the slight tenting of the material. A blush stained her cheeks as she looked up and caught him staring at her, a knowing look in his eyes. Brushing a lock of hair back from her face, she focused on a spot just over his shoulder.

He had to have known the effect those jeans would have on her. If fact, she would have bet on it. Ryan in a tailored suit was gorgeous, but in relaxed clothing – jeans specifically – he was almost irresistible. Despite their sexual power dynamics, she had been known to jump him when he would come into a room wearing just his jeans.

Forcing herself back to the here and now, where he was waiting on an answer to his question she shook her head no. She wasn't certain she could count a granola bar and a cup of coffee as a meal, but it was all she had been able to force down. Her throat had felt too tight to swallow anything anyways.

Ryan stepped forward and cupped her chin, forcing her to look at him. His head tipped down, and he pressed his lips to hers, softly, tenderly. Erika wanted to wrap her arms around his neck and lose herself in the sensation. At the same time she wanted to shove him away and storm out. As his lips moved over her cheek and down her neck, she tipped her head back, and just let herself feel.

She was to be his for the next two days, and despite her hatred for his actions, she realized she still cared, which made her heart ache.

Closing her eyes, she relaxed against him as she came to the determination that this time, she would use him. She'd get her grandmother's painting for free, letting him foot the bill, and in the end, she'd walk away from him and not look back. She'd hurt him as he had her, as he still was. Because she was quickly realizing this weekend might very well succeed in tearing her heart out, just when she had started thinking about moving on.

In what time she had with him, she was going to enjoy the masterful way he could play her body, drawing forth sensations no other man had managed, storing up the memories for when they parted again. When it didn't hurt so much, she would pull the memories out again, and savor them. As much as she knew being a submissive was an integral part of herself, Erica doubted she would ever find another lover that she fit with as well as she did with Ryan.

As if he sensed her thoughts weren't completely with him in the present, Ryan's hand fisted in her hair and with a soft jerk, he forced her head forward, causing her eyes to fly open. Almost savagely, he kissed her, thrusting his tongue into her mouth as he used his other hand to pull her tight against his body, the hardness of his cock pressing against her stomach.

Shifting back and forth, she rubbed her nipples against the warmth of his smooth chest, her pussy growing moist with the tactile touch of his body against hers. His free hand grabbed her ass, pulling her tight against him. The hand in her hair tightened, and he broke the kiss. Tipping his head, he nipped at her neck, sending a sharp jolt of pain straight to her nipples. Shivering at the dual sensations, she wanted to curl up inside of his body and never come out. Her body missed his, and she hadn't had a clue how much until this moment.

His fingers, torturously slow, started their trek around her body, dancing over every erogenous zone along the way, until they slipped between her legs and cupped her sex. Erika trembled as he stroked a fingertip along the seam of her pussy lips, then delved inside. She knew he could feel how wet she was for him, and she flushed in embarrassment. She wanted to hate him, wanted to hate his touch, but her body was alive with need for him. It remembered his touch, and the masterful way he could bring her to pleasure.

Bastard that he was, she knew he wasn't above using it to his advantage. She had no doubt she would find fulfillment with him, his ego would demand nothing less than that she come apart in his arms.

As he stroked along her inner walls, a second fingertip joined the first, curling slightly inside of her body, caressing her slick flesh. Erika gasped as he thrust them hard inside of her, the hand in her hair tightening as he pulled her head back and bit the side of her neck.

Trembling in his arms, her body betraying her, she could feel her juices trickling down her inner thighs as her anticipation built. It had been so long since she had been touched. Her body was responding to each brush of his skin against hers, each stroke of his fingertip as he pumped his two fingers into her pussy, then pulled them out, only to thrust them in again.

Whimpering as her orgasm built, she bit her lip, trying to delay the inevitable.

"You know you want to come, Erika. Why fight it?" Her eyes flew open at his words. He hadn't given her permission to come, and she had fallen back into the pattern of waiting for it. Satisfaction glinted in his eyes, mixed with something close to regret. Shaking off the fanciful notion that Ryan Carstairs had anything to feel guilty about, especially since this was his doing, Erica closed her eyes and arched into his touch, grinding her pubic bone against his palm as she reached for the release. A release her brain refused her.

Her nerves wound tighter, her pussy contracting around his fingers, her body demanding the release from the pressure, but she couldn't come. Her eyes flew open in frustration.

A humorless chuckle passed Ryan's lips, and then he whispered those sweet words her ears had grown to miss, "Come for me."

The world flew apart as her orgasm crashed over her. Breathless, she collapsed against his chest, trusting him to keep her from falling, as he had so many times before.

When reality returned, she focused her gaze on his chest as she awaited his next order. Her fingers itched to explore his body, remembering familiar and beloved patterns of touch. It was torture for her to be this close to him. It seemed to be a mockery of what they had shared. But if she closed her eyes and stopped thinking, she could almost fool herself into believing it was real, that the months of loneliness had been a bad dream.

"Touch me," he growled against her neck.

She reached between them and grasped the snap of his pants, undoing it and sliding her hands past the waist and down his body. Stroking her hands along his pelvis, she moved her way to his groin. Stroking one hand up and down his cock, she cupped his balls with her other. Almost as if her fingers moved of their own violation, they stroked him in remembered patterns, slipping past the ring of his ass and gently stroking over the ball of nerves just inside his ass.

He pulled his hand from her pussy and cupped her right leg, coaxing it up and around his waist. His cock brushed against her smooth shaven skin as it sought entrance to her core. He rocked his hips, gliding his cock back and forth, coating it in the cream that still trickled from her body, evidence of her desire for him.

Unable to hold back, she whispered his name softly, her body craving the feel of his cock sliding deep within her, filling her as only he ever had.

With a muffled curse, he dropped her leg and pulled away. His pants pulled down around his hips, his cock swaying free, he awkwardly stalked away from her. Erika quickly adjusted her stance to catch her balance. Running a hand through his hair, he used his other to pull up his pants.

Erika stood motionless, watching him as he headed out of the room, only to return a few moments later with her clothing. Tossing it at her feet, he said, "The painting's yours. Get dressed, grab it and get out. I'll have the limo brought around for you."

"I don't understand." Ignoring the clothing at her feet, she tried to understand his sudden mood change.

"I can't do this any more. Just go." Ryan dropped into the chair next to her, and leaned back, closing his eyes. Watching a defeated look come over his features, Erika moved closer and nudged him with her foot. When he opened his eyes and looked at her, she met his gaze head on. His eyes glistened with moisture, and for a moment she wondered if it was tears, before she shrugged the thought of that possibility aside as highly unlikely.

"What changed?"

"Damn it, woman, can't you take a hint?"

"Why did you break off the engagement?"

As his eyes widened, Erika knew she had hit a nerve. She hadn't intended to ask, and if she was smart, she'd grab the painting and run, but the look on his face was unlike any she had seen before. It scared her, how much it hurt seeing him looking like that. She ached to make him better.

"You don't know?"

She shook her head, wondering why he would think she would.

"I know you got my letter. I sent it certified and got a receipt back."

Remembering the envelope sitting unopened in the back of her closet, she wished in that moment to have it in her hands. Suddenly, she was dying to know what it said.

"I got it, I just never read it."

"Fuck!" Ryan exclaimed, his breath rushing out of him. Leaning forward, he set his elbows on his knees and watched her as he spoke slowly. "So you had no idea that I begged you to understand, that I explained everything about the engagement. How Cindy was desperate, how she just found out her father was dying of cancer and he wanted her taken care of, and how he always looked to me to do that. How she sent out the announcement, figuring I would support her, and pretend for the few weeks that remained of her father's life, since she couldn't tell him that she was already in love...with another woman. She was afraid the news would send him to his grave either mad at her or earlier than expected."

The world dropped out from under Erika's feet. She collapsed on the hardwood floor, her bare ass against the cool wood. Reeling from the news, she didn't know what to say. A whole year she had hated Ryan for lying to her, and then to find out that he never had.

"Why the painting then?"

Ryan laughed softly, the mocking sound echoing in the still room. "I tried to forget you, to tell myself that you obviously weren't worth the effort, if you couldn't understand the desperation Cindy felt. I waited until the week after the funeral to send the letter, knowing you might need time to cool down and be willing to listen to me. So I waited to send it, then after I did I waited another week, and tried to call you. You wouldn't take my call, so I waited another week, then two, then a month, hoping you would finally call me. Waiting for you to reach out to me.

"When I saw the auction, I remembered you and your mom trying to get all the paintings back. I got hold of the list of items up for sale, and when I saw the painting, I started thinking I could get you back in my life through it. I was going to seduce you, remind you how good it was between us, hopefully make you want to stay, and if you still hated me, then I'd walk away like you did. But I couldn't do it."

Feeling the sting of tears in her eyes, Erika blinked rapidly, her chest tight at the pain in Ryan's voice. Her proud lover, the strongest man she had ever met seemed lost. Looking into his misery-filled eyes, she couldn't stand the distance between them any more. Her nature demanded she comfort him.

She ached to hold him pressed tight against her chest, to stroke her hands up and down his back as she soothed the pain away, but feared that he wouldn't welcome it. Not because he didn't want her touch, but because of the man he was; the strong dominant personality traits that she loved so much made it hard to know just what would comfort and what would offend him, even if only subconsciously.

Climbing to her feet, she closed the distance between them and knelt between his parted legs. As his eyes lightened, more of the man she knew him to be returning, she had an idea of what to do to completely ease him. Her hands lifted to the snap of his jeans. Ryan jerked as she pulled the material down, baring his cock. Slowly, she tipped her head and laid her face against his inner thigh, her breath whispering across his flesh.

She held herself motionless for an eternity, fearing she had made a mistake. She wanted to show him her devotion, to remind him that he was strong. Eternity passed until his hands settled on top of her head and he stroked his fingers through her hair. She wanted to do more, but it wasn't her way to initiate. As it was, she had stepped outside of her bounds with him, but hoped he would understand the nature of her offering. Kneeling before him was the ultimate submission she could make. Pressing her bare skin against his the ultimate comfort she was able to offer.

She could hear the gentle rasp of his breath in the stillness of the living room as he stroked her hair, smoothing the strands along her shoulders. He slid his hand down her neck, and gently pushed against the line of her spine until her lips pressed against his cock. She could pull away; his touch was light enough she had complete choice and could stop this at any moment.

Instead, she opened her mouth and sucked the tip in and worshiped him with her tongue, rolling it over the slit and down along the edge of the sensitive bulb. His hand fisted in her hair as his hips lifted, guiding more of his length into her mouth.

Sucking him deep, she applied all of her skill to showing him her forgiveness, knowing if she tried to tell him how she felt while they were both still reeling it could potentially backfire. He knew her body better than she did. Naked before him, she was an open book; all he had to do was read what was there.

Just kneeling before him, she knew she had showed him something. It implied a trust. He was the first man she had completely submitted to, and the first night that she had knelt before him, and allowed her hands to be cuffed to her ankles, her neck wrapped in a collar, she had shown him the depth of those feelings. He had fucked her mouth that night, the first time he had come without bringing her to orgasm first, and she had reveled in the sensation of his juices flowing down her throat, knowing she had brought him to that pleasure.

That night, after hours spent tied to the bed, being driven to orgasm after orgasm, until her body couldn't take anymore, she had curled up against his side and slid down in the bed. Sucking his cock into her mouth, she had suckled him until she had drifted to sleep. The next morning she had woken up to find his cock hard and still in her mouth. As soon as he had noticed she was awake, Ryan had started to rock softly against her until he had climaxed, his come warm and welcome in her mouth. She had swallowed all of his gift, savoring the taste of his passion.

Now, she hoped to rekindle that, as they both forgave and moved past the hurt. Heart aching, knowing it would take time to rebuild what they had, she offered all of herself as she serviced him, her mouth bringing him pleasure.

When she felt him throbbing, his cock jerking as his pre-cum leaked down her throat, she waited, silently offering to swallow if he wished to come in her mouth. As he pulled back, she became aware of the throbbing between her own legs, the need to be filled by him. Her nipples ached to be played with, either rolled gently between his thumb and forefinger or pinched between the jaws of a gator clamp. Her ass-ring contracted, aching just as much as her pussy.

"Stand up."

Her legs shaking, Erika stood before him, wondering how he was going to take her, or if that was his plan. She stepped back when he stood. Carefully, his hands cupped her shoulders, and guided her down until she was sitting in the chair. Then he knelt before her and smoothed his hands over her knees and lower legs. There were a few red marks from the floor, but nothing too uncomfortable.

With soft presses of his lips, he kissed each one before standing in front of her. "Kiss me," he commanded. Her lips curled into a smile of pure devilment, Erica leaned forward and did as he commanded, her lips wet and soft against his stomach. She delighted in the growl that Ryan responded with.

He didn't stop her, but she could see his hands clenching into fists at his side as he allowed her to play. After a year apart, and more heartache that she would even have imagined they were capable of dealing to each other, she needed this playful moment to help her regain her balance.

As much as she needed to show him her submission, she also needed to rekindle the simple joy being with him generated. Nipping lightly at his stomach, she slowly worked her way down to the fly of his jeans where she waited, her breath whispering softly over his cock.

Instead of fisting his hands in her hair, or demanding she suck him into her mouth, Ryan leaned down and wrapped his arms around her, holding her tight against his body. She could feel his heart beating an erratic pace against his chest, her own responding in kind. Tears stung the backs of her eyes, but she forced them to not fall by blinking, and finally closing her eyes.

At his whispered words, "My heart", the last year of pain melted away.

As Ryan slowly released her and stood back up, she looked up, staring into love filled eyes. He held his hands out, and as she clasped them, he pulled her up and against his body. With her pressed against his chest, he slid down his jeans and kicked them off, then sat back down in the chair.

Rather than coax her to her knees again, Ryan clasped her hips in his warm hands, turning her around and pulling her down onto his lap. Straddling him, Erika gasped at the delicious feel of his cock along the cleft of her pussy, stroking along the sensitive folds.

He kissed her, and it felt like coming home after a long trip. The velvety feel his tongue sliding against hers wiped away the pain of his earlier brutal kisses. The delicate probing of his fingers on her labia as he readied her for his cock set her pulse to racing. When the surge of his cock slid deep inside of her, she felt as if the entire world had ceased to exist, except them.

Rocking forward, she welcomed him into her body. His grip tightly dug into her hips and she reveled in the knowledge that in the morning she would be marked by his passion. It didn't matter if it was stripes from a whip or the subtle imprint of his fingers. What mattered was wearing the marking of his possession.

She relaxed her body, allowing him to guide her motions, rocking her back and forth, guiding her up and down on him, driving them both together into euphoria. When he tore his lips away she whimpered softly, her body needing more.

"Pinch your nipples," he ordered, his voice hoarse.

Smiling softly, Erika reached between them and grasped her nipples between her thumbs and forefingers, pinching as hard as she could stand, then applying a twist. Pain shot down to her clit, sending a spasm through her pussy.

Moaning softly, she arched her back, clenching her slick inner muscles around the thick shaft of his cock. The feel of him buried in her was intoxicating. It had been so very long. She hadn't been with another man, nor allowed herself even the feel of a vibrator, knowing it couldn't recreate what Ryan could. It had been simply better to go without.

"Harder," he growled.

Erika tightened her hold, her body screaming inwardly, protesting the discomfort. As a reward Ryan slid a hand between them, pinching and pulling at her clit while he continued to guide the motion of her body.

Erika could feel the faint first twinges of her orgasm and clenched as hard as she could around him, remembering all the times she had been gagged, unable to signal that she was so close, so she had shown Ryan with her body.

A soft groan answered her, as he started rocked harder against her, thrusting his hips up, driving his cock deep into her core. His grip on her hips tightened as he forcefully pulled her down against him, pinching her clit harder than she was her own nipples.

"Who do you belong to?"

Erika gasped as he pulled at her clit, stretching the tiny bundle of nerves in a deliciously painful way.

"You," she panted, needing to come, but knowing she had to hold back. Her orgasm wasn't hers, it was his to allow her.

"Say it. Say that you're mine."

"I'm yours, Ryan. My body, my heart, they're yours to use as you will."

His lips slammed down against hers, his tongue mirroring the motions of his cock as he ground her harder against him. Erika wanted to sob with frustration as she held off her orgasm, her body spiraling higher and higher, seeking the euphoric release. Nerves tight, she clenched him as tight within her as she could, silently begging for his permission. She felt as if she would go mad if he didn't give it.

As he broke the kiss, she moaned, her eyes closed tight.

"Come for me," he whispered, so softly she wasn't certain she heard him. Opening her eyes, she stared into his as he ordered, "Show me your body is mine. Come for me."

She gave a soft scream as her orgasm claimed her, taking her slightly by surprise at the force of it. She could feel Ryan's thrusts growing erratic as he surged against her, then jerked, his grip holding her motionless as his cock bucked inside of her, his come mingling with her juices.

Breathless, she released her grip on her nipples and collapsed against him, needing to feel the heat of his body against hers.

* * *

Almost a week later, as soon as the shower came on, Erika climbed out of her bed and opened the closet door. When they had arrived at her place the night before so she could grab a few things to move to his place, the lure of the bed had been too strong to resist. They had ended up making love until they both fell asleep.

Pushing her clothing aside she grabbed the box that held all of his gifts she had saved. Grabbing it, she climbed back onto the bed and opened it, her pulse racing. Carefully, she lifted out the box that contained the jewelry, the rose petals she had painstakingly dried and wrapped in bubble wrap, the lingerie, and other beloved items. Holding her jeweled collar in her hands, she rubbed her thumbs over it, stroking the smooth silver, inhaling the slightly acrid scent of the metal. Her fingertips brushed over the smaller inset jewels, which she and Ryan had painstakingly selected together, picking out ones that matched each of their eyes colors.

Lifting it to her neck, she clasped it and centered it, so that her name was in front, resting under her chin. The cold metal heated with the warmth of her skin, settling comfortably, like it was only yesterday she had worn it for him.

Fingers trembling, she reached back into the box for the letter and lifted it out. The lettering on the envelope had faded slightly, but she could still make out her name and address, written in Ryan's precise handwriting. Tracing the letters with her fingertip, she put off the inevitable until she couldn't stand it any longer.

Opening the seal, she pulled the stationary out and set the envelope back into the box. As she started reading tears shimmered in her eyes and blazed a heated trail along her cheeks, but she ignored them. All that mattered were the words on the page, words that poured from the heart of her beloved.

As she came to the last line, a sob escaped her and the letter fluttered to the mattress. Holding her palm against her heart, she tried to bring her racing emotions under control, and hadn't noticed the silence of the shower.

The sound of Ryan's voice had her turning guiltily, a blush staining her cheeks as she faced him.

"I still mean it."

Erika held out her hand for Ryan's, pulling him down for a kiss, then she laid her face against his chest, his heartbeat a soothing rhythm as she struggled to control her need for him.

Gently, he cupped her chin and tipped her face up, forcing her to look into his eyes. The love shining back at her as he traced his fingertip over the engravings in the collar around her throat caused her chest to tightened, her heart to race. Throat dry, she swallowed heavily, waiting for him to say something more, uncertain what to say herself.

"I still want to marry you. I came home that day with a ring in my pocket, hoping to claim you for my own, and then I was going to explain what Cindy had done. I had faith you would understand why Cindy have been forced to such a rash action, that you would even support the need for such a deception given your gentle heart. When I saw the newspaper on the table and you packing, I didn't know what to do, what to say. I had the evening planned out perfectly, then things suddenly went to hell.

"I wanted to do it different this time, but I guess planning isn't going to work. It's not really our style anyways. So, forget all the rest of it, will you marry me?"

Flinging her arms around his neck, Erika held tight to him, hoping she wouldn't wake up from the dream. "Yes," she whispered against his neck, the sound coming out more of a croak as it slid past her tight throat.

Pulling back, she looked into his eyes, and climbed off the bed. Kneeling down before him, she laid her head against his inner thigh, her mouth a breath away from his cock.

A flash of gold caught her attention as the curtains flickered, letting the sunlight in. Looking over Ryan's thigh, she couldn't help admiring the beauty of the painting hanging on the wall. Erika felt tears welling in her eyes, tears of thanks for her grandmother, and her unashamed acceptance of the breathtaking quality of passion.

She only wished she had the talent to add a second painting of her and Ryan, one of this very moment, forever capturing her complete trust and submission. Almost as if Ryan knew what she was thinking, a hand dropped to her head and she could feel it trembling as he brushed the strands of her hair before trailing down her neck to rest on her collar.

* * *

The story is not over yet. Continue reading for a glimpse into Ryan and Erica's life before their breakup.

LOVE SLAVE

Erika closed her eyes and rocked back against Ryan as he slowly thrust forward, driving his cock hard and deep into her pussy. Whimpering softly as he slowly slid back out, she fought the urge to beg him to let her come. Gripping the back of the chair so tightly her knuckles turned white, she held her ground even as her legs trembled.

Ryan chuckled softly in her ear, his voice deep and so perfect as he whispered, "You feel so good baby, so damn tight and hot. Clench for me. Tighten those slick muscles around me."

His hands grasped her hips firmly, holding her steady against him as he slowly the pace to a tortuously slow grind. Her body screamed for an orgasm, but he hadn't told her she could, and she wasn't about to disappoint him. Biting her bottom lip, she clenched her core tight around his hardness, attempting to hold him tight within her body.

Ryan rewarded her with a hard thrust, his balls slapping against her ass as he pulled back and thrust again. Her breasts jerked with the force, nipples brushing against the soft material covering the chair.

"That's good baby. I know you want to come, don't you?"

Erika nodded, unable to speak. Her nerves were so sensitive from his drawn out seduction that each glide of his body against hers was almost painful it felt so good. Even the thin layer of the gauzy gown her had her wear for him was agonizing. The material was bunched at her waist, leaving her entire lower body bare, and open to Ryan's touch. The laces at the front had been undone, her breasts hanging free.

She could feel the heat of his chest through the material, the weight of his body against hers a welcome feeling. She loved the feel of his body, his masterful touch as he claimed her body, proving to her the she was his--body and heart.

Ryan groaned behind her as he picked up the pace of his thrusts, a silent signal that he was close to his own orgasm. Whimpering softly, Erika prayed that he would allow her to come. All day he had played with her body, teasing her nipples, burying his fingers in her pussy, tonguing her clit, and even whipping her butt with his favorite flogger, each time pushing her just to the edge of orgasm but not letting her crest.

All week she had been his slave, wearing only the thin gowns he had provided, her body open to his touch at any moment. Her breasts were still tender from yesterday's gift, a set of nipple clamps with varying attachable weights.

Rather than celebrate Valentine's Day as one event, Ryan had spent a week leading up to it, and now that the day was here, Erika didn't know if she was going to survive it. Already she was pushed beyond what she had previously seen as her limits, and she didn't know if the end was in sight, but she was loving every minute of it. Every slow glide of his cock in her pussy or ass, ever pinch of nipple clamps, every whip and paddle against her ass or pussy, every thrust of his cock in her mouth, every sensual torture Ryan dished out.

Ryan's hand slipped down between her body and the chair. His nimble fingers reached her clit and started to roll the tiny ball of nerves between his thumb and forefinger before giving it a hard pinch. Erika gasped softly, her head dropping back to rest on Ryan's shoulder as he drove harder against her. Gripping the chair tight, she pushed the orgasm back, even as it threatened to overwhelm her.

"That's good baby, I can feel your pussy quivering around me, your body trembling as you wait for me to allow your orgasm. I'm so proud of you baby."

Erika whimpered, her breath coming in fast pants as she fought to deserve his praise. It was so hard, her juices were a steady stream down her thighs as he pounded against her.

"You can come now," he whispered, so softly Erika doubted she had heard correctly. Rolling her head back and forth on his shoulder, she struggled to quiet the dull roar in her ears as he spoke again. "That's right Erika. Your body's mine, your orgasm's mine. Come for me."

Her heart racing, Erika released the tight control she had on her body and let the waves of her orgasm crest. They swept over her, she fast and deep, she felt like she was drowning. Ryan's hands on her hips held her steady though, and she let the sensations claim her, knowing he would keep her safe.

Almost from a distance, she heard Ryan groan, then the warm flood of his come within her as he climaxed.

Legs trembling, she leaned forward over the chair, her body limp and unable to take any more. Feeling completely wrung out, she only managed a faint whimper of protest as Ryan's cock slipped form her body and he moved from around behind her.

Gently he brushed her sweaty hair back from her forehead, and trialed his fingertips down her face and neck.

"You did good baby, so very good."

Erika smiled softly, knowing he could see her adoration in her eyes.

"It's time for your last gift."

A surge of anticipating pushed her weariness to the background as he picked up a small package from the seat of the chair. Rather than hand it to her, he opened the lid and showed her what was inside--a silver collar, her name engraved in a sweeping font, the letters curling gracefully.

As Ryan grabbed the collar and tossed the box aside, she found herself holding her breath. The feel of the metal against her sweat soaked skin made the moment more real. It wasn't a soft glide of a necklace chain, rather it was a study reminder of Ryan's possession, of his claim to her and her place in his life.

"We'll go tomorrow and pick out stones to adorn it with, ones to match the color of your eyes."

As the clasp snapped into place, she raised trembling fingers to trace her name.

"And yours too," she answered, affirming the commitment accepting the collar implied. She wanted the jewelry to contain a piece of both of them. Ryan's fingers brushed against hers, and with tears of joy in her eyes she tipped her head up for his kiss.

Ryan whispered one word against her lips before claiming her mouth. "Mine."

A SECOND CHANCE AT LOVE

* * *

HER BEST MAN

Disheartened, Katherine slumped to the kitchen floor and stared at the filled boxes surrounding her. It was sad to see three and a half years of her life reduced to a couple dozen boxes. She could see the corner of a picture frame peeking out from one box, her clothing tossed haphazardly into another few. Most of the things that had been part of her home, she had to leave behind.

"Damn him," she whispered to the empty room.

Not one to normally sit and cry over what couldn't be changed, she blinked rapidly as her eyes started to burn, heralding tears to come. Wiping angrily at her eyes with the backs of her hands, she refused to let them fall. Grabbing another of the boxes, she folded the flaps down and taped them closed, before pushing it aside.

The quick rap of knuckles against her kitchen door was the only warning she had before Rick swung the door open and stepped into the room. The sunlight glinted off his sandy hair, catching on the blond highlights and creating a slight halo effect before the door swung closed behind him.

"Hey, gorgeous," he said as he squatted next to her. "Ready to move into your new place and leave the shit-head a mess?"

Despite the urge to cry, Katherine couldn't resist laughing. "He's your best friend, Rick. Even though you're my friend, even though my marriage ended, I don't want to come between you two. You were the best man at our wedding, for crying out loud."

"Babe, you're not making me choose. *He did*, the moment he cheated on you. Especially since he actually had the nerve to expect me to cover for him."

Katherine felt a tingle inside at the touch of his warm hand as he cupped her cheek and tipped her head up, forcing her gaze to meet his. "He's also not worth crying over."

She wanted to drown in the warmth of his blue eyes, to curl up inside of him and sleep until the pain disappeared.

"I know." And she did. As much as Brian had hurt her, she knew he wasn't worth it. She knew when she married him that he was immature despite how much she thought he loved her. She didn't expect to change him, but she had expected him to settle down like he swore he would.

That promise, like so many others, had long since been broken. Rick knew about the cheating, but he had no idea about the other issues that had plagued their brief marriage—the gambling and the drinking were what worried her most. She left him before she found herself in debt, and before his drunken rages had escalated into full-on abuse. The other women just made the decision easier.

"I still think you should have kept the house in the divorce. You gave in much too easily, asking only to live here until everything was finalized."

"Yeah, well, I didn't want the constant reminders." Needing to stop that train of thought before she pictured the image of her husband and his latest bimbo in their bed, she quickly changed the subject. "I think I'm about done, and since you're so determined to help, you can go ahead and start tossing the boxes in my car."

"Yes, ma'am." Rick pressed a brief kiss against her forehead then stood. Katherine watched him stack two boxes, pick them up, and head out to the door. Shaking her head, she pushed how good the feel of his lips against her skin had felt aside and focused on getting the rest of her stuff into boxes. The last thing she needed at the moment was to remember her hopes of getting together with him before she was swept off her feet by his best friend. Where Rick was steady and calm, patient to a fault, and the best friend she could ever ask for, Brian had been a whirlwind of intensity, leaving her unbalanced, heart racing, and ready to go at a moment's notice. She often wondered what would have been if she had tried with Rick instead, if she had been able to get him to see her as something other than his friend.

Would they have a kid by now? Would he be cheating? Would she? Or would they be looking forward to what the future held for them?

Eyes burning with a fresh rush of tears, this time self-pitying and mocking, she blinked rapidly and turned her attention back to her task—packing all her things and starting over.

She was taping the last of her boxes about twenty minutes later when Rick squatted next to her again. "Okay, so far we have loaded your car and most of my truck cab with your stuff, but the bed's still halfway empty. Anything else you want to take with you?"

Katherine looked through the doorway to the living room, painstakingly decorated, each piece debated over as she tried to mesh her and Brian's style together. There were a few pieces she liked, but nothing she loved—not as she had the cherry coffee-table, or the sleigh bed, or the dozen other pieces she had resisted the urge to buy in favor of something Brian would also like.

Every item of furniture only reminded her of how much she had compromised, and how little of herself had shown through in their marriage. She planned to buy all of the things she had wanted in the first place, to furnish her new place.

"No, nothing. I'll just grab my laptop bag, and if you'll get this box, we're ready to go."

"Tell you what, hon, I'll grab both and you walk through again, just in case. We can pad the big-screen if you want it, or I can find someone to help get the fridge or even the washer and dryer into the truck bed if you'd like. Just think about it." Katherine smiled just as she knew Rick had planned it out. She hadn't planned on him helping, but should have. He had been considerate throughout the last few months, stopping by often to check on her, always leaving her with a vaguely frustrated feeling as he left. She yearned for him, in a way she shouldn't have. Deep inside, she couldn't help but wonder if that was what had driven Brian to cheat, to drink and gamble, because although she was faithful to him in body, her soul craved the man she had walked away from years ago.

As Rick headed out with his last load, Katherine stood and walked through the house for the last time, the ghosts of the past trailing behind her. Some of her friends had told her she should take Brian to the cleaners, get the house and everything in it, but she had settled for a quick divorce. He had moved into a hotel during the three months required to be considered separated to push the proceedings forward. This morning they had signed the last of the paperwork. In the eyes of the courts, and everyone else, their relationship was officially over. But standing there in the house, she could feel the memories pressing in on her.

Brushing at a tear that had escaped, she wondered just how trapped he had felt the last few months they were together. Certainly she had felt it for a while, and given they hadn't slept together in the same room for more than the last two months of their marriage she wondered why she hadn't filed sooner. She had thought about it frequently, but always put it down that he needed her. Maybe it was her fault.

Signing softly, she trailed a finger over the faint coating of dust that had accumulated on the banister in the last few days. The house did hold some good memories. Brian carrying her up the stairs on their anniversary, their first night in their own home. One afternoon when he had been out of town for a few days, and he came home early, they had made love in the entryway. The long dinners, where they had sat and talked for hours. The bubble-baths together.

Each step easier to take than the last, she climbed the stair case and walked down the hall, until she stood in the bedroom doorway. Leaning against the doorframe, she stood there in silence and let the tears win. As the heat of them trailed down her cheeks, rolling along the line of her jaw until they landed with a wet splash against her shirt, she remembered the good and the bad times.

Being chased around the room until he tumbled them both onto the bed, where they had screwed each other senseless.

The sight of him on top of some nameless blonde, his lean hips pumping as he groaned out his ecstasy. Him drinking himself senseless and stumbling to bed.

A throat clearing behind her had her jerking away from the doorway and turning. Rick stood near the top of the stairs, a hesitant look on his face. "I didn't want to bother you, but you've been standing there almost a half hour, and I started to get worried."

As his gaze flowed over her face, his eyes darkened and he climbed the last few steps. His hands cupped her cheeks, and calloused thumbs brushed the tear stains from them.

"Are you sure?" Rick asked. "Are you ready to move out and move on?"

Katherine nodded, her throat too tight to speak. It wasn't that she didn't want to leave Brian behind. She just didn't know what the future held anymore, and the urge to stay where she felt comfortable, even if she wasn't happy, was strong. A small part of her screamed for her to call Brian up and work things out, damn the divorce. Yet looking into Rick's eyes, she reclaimed the core of strength within her that had been holding her steady. She deserved better than Brian, and even if his unhappiness was partially her fault, it was also his for not asking to be let go. In that, she wouldn't suffer the blame.

"I'm ready. It's time to go."

Stepping back, she pulled away from Rick's touch before she did something stupid, and shifted past him and headed down to the first floor. She could hear the quiet tread of his boots on the steps behind her.

Without pausing, she tossed her keys on the hallway table, headed into the kitchen and out the door. Rick followed, stopping long enough to turn the lock on the door and pull it closed. She headed to her car and was sinking into the seat before she started shaking.

Rick's gaze met hers as he headed to his truck, and he winked at her. Despite the pain, the fear bombarding her, she smiled back. It hurt, but having Rick steady beside her, knowing he would be with her through this, helped. During the months of separation, she had steadily lost most of her friends as they were "couple" friends—and they didn't know how to relate to her now that she wasn't part of the couple. Only Rick seemed to be able to adjust to her being single, to her being without Brian. She wasn't certain if it was because he knew her before, or if it was due to his anger at Brian. Whatever it was, though, she was grateful to have him to lean on.

* * *

Several days later, Katherine had just settled down on her newly bought couch in her now decorated apartment, when a knock sounded at the door. Kicking off her shoes as she stood, she moved to the door and looked out the peephole. Rick stood on the other side, his sandy hair slightly curly and unruly.

Running a hand through her auburn locks, trying to bring them to some semblance of order, she waited for him to knock again before opening the door. With a grin, Rick held up a pizza box perfectly balanced on one hand and used his other to pull her close for a hug. Katherine allowed herself the brief touch of her body against his, the moment to inhale the scent of his cologne and slightly sweaty skin, and then pulled back.

"Welcome to my abode." Stepping back, she grabbed the pizza and headed into the kitchen. She caught a glimpse of Rick grabbing something off the floor at his feet before following her into the apartment.

Katherine set the pizza down on the counter, then turned around, watching Rick take in her new place. His knowing gaze trailed over the furniture as he surveyed the room, a smile curving his lips. When he reached her, she could feel the liquid heat of his gaze trailing over her, before meeting her eyes. "Now this is more you," he said as he crossed the room and slipped past her. After setting the bag down on the counter, he started searching through the cabinets.

"Make yourself at home." Katherine drawled, amused rather than upset at his highhandedness. He was just Rick. Given all the years she had known him, she wouldn't have expected anything else but that he make himself comfortable in her home.

As he pulled down two of her long-stemmed wine glasses, she couldn't help herself. Peering into the bag, she saw a nice Merlot, her favorite wine. Knowing Rick was more of a beer drinker when he was in the mood for alcohol, she had to give him credit. Pizza and a nice glass, or two, of wine was her perfect relaxing evening.

"How did you know I hadn't eaten?"

Rick turned toward her, set the glasses on the counter, and stepped close, pressing her back against the edge between him and the bottle of wine. He braced one hand on the counter at her hip and reached for the wine with his other, and for a brief moment Katherine felt the glide of his body against hers. Her nipples hardened in response to the feel of his chest separated only by a few layers of clothing. "I know you like to eat around seven."

Katherine tried to remember what they were talking about, but couldn't. She felt like she had licked her finger and touched it to a live wire.

She watched Rick's eyes darken, and his Adam's apple lift up then drop as he swallowed. The tension in the room thickened, and she couldn't help leaning towards him, brushing her body against his again, subconsciously teasing them both. When they were hanging out it was something she had always wanted to do, but she always figured he would make the first move if he wanted to take things from friendship to something more. When he never did, she cut her loses and looked elsewhere, managing to keep him in her life as her friend.

Nostrils flaring with each deep breath he took, Rick set the bottle back down, stepped back and freed her. Rather than move away, Katherine moved closer and tentatively clasped his shoulders. Rick's head tipped towards hers, his lids opening softly. Looking into his smoky eyes, she couldn't help wondering what the hell she ever saw in her ex. This man was the one who fired her blood, and now at least he seemed to know it.

As his lips brushed against hers, she slid her arms around his neck and pressed closer. Opening her mouth, she invited his tongue to sweep past her lips and engage her own in a duel for control. His hands grasped her hips and pulled her tight against his body, the counter pressed hard against her back, but she didn't care. All that mattered was his fingers slowly working her skirt up higher and higher, until the top of her thighs were exposed. The feel of his fingertips gently stroking her skin was unlike Brian's touch. Where Brain had been quick to passion, quick to feed her own need, and quick to seek their mutual completion, Rick was slowly stoking the fires within her, coaxing her a bit at a time.

Sliding a leg to the side, she managed to straddle one of his firm thighs, and gasped as he pressed it tight against her crotch, grinding in to the sensitive skin covered by a wisp of lace and cotton.

Fisting her hands in the material of his shirt, she squirmed against him, causing him to lift her higher against him, until her toes barely touched the floor. His hands slid to her ass, cupping the sensitive cheeks and raised her up onto the countertop, all without breaking their kiss.

Katherine gasped in his mouth as he shifted their position, pressing his denim clad crotch against hers, teasing her with the delicious friction as he rocked slowly back and forth, the flow of his body ebbing just when she craved it the most.

Breaking the kiss, she tipped her head to the side as his head dipped, his lips pressed against her rapidly beating pulse. "This is crazy," she whispered.

Rick's lips left her neck from one heartbeat to the next, and he moved back. Tensing, she lifted her head and opened her eyes to look at him. He was breathing heavily, looking for all the world like a man fighting a battle within himself.

"I didn't say I didn't want this, just that it's crazy."

"I'm taking advantage of you," he responded.

Katherine grabbed hold of his shirt and pulled him closer, succeeding only by catching him off guard. "No, you're not. You never did. I waited weeks for you to show you were ready to move beyond friends, lonely nights, wondering if I was reading your signals wrong, too scared to trust myself enough to make the first move."

Rick's eyes widened for a moment, before a small smile curved his lips. "And here I thought you didn't see me that way. Every time I worked up the nerve to make a move, you always seemed to withdraw."

"I was scared, Rick. I wanted you, but I was scared of what you made me feel." She could feel the beat of his heart under her knuckles, the steady thump-thump at sharp contrast to her own racing pulse. She had always admired that about him, his ability to be in such control of himself, yet so free.

He reminded her of a wild animal, managing to function within society, but always drawn elsewhere. Where Brian was outgoing and reckless, Rick had always been steady, with a leashed intensity she was only now coming to understand.

"So much lost time," he whispered as he leaned down, the brush of his lips over hers so light, she wondered if she had imagined it, until he brushed over them again. As he passed by a third time, she licked her lips as his were passing over.

Rick groaned softly and shifted closer, but still not close enough for her. Sliding her feet up the side of his legs, she wrapped them around his waist and locked her ankles, forcing him back in the cradle of her body. The thought of dinner brushed briefly against her mind, but the feel of his body against her was more important than any pizza ever could be. There was a microwave, and reheated pizza was almost as good as it was fresh.

"We have a lot of catching up to do," she whispered against his lips before claiming them with her tongue, thrusting past and deepening their chaste kiss into one of carnal delight. Her fingers trembling with the intensity of her need for him, Katherine grasped the bottom of his shirt and pulled it free of his jeans. Rich groaned and broke the kiss, his hands unsteady as he helped her pull the shirt over his head. As she tossed it aside, his fingers tangled in her auburn hair, gently tugging until she tipped her head back, allowing him access to her neck.

Her motions jerky, she managed to get the first two buttons undone, but his lips quickly followed, placing soft open-mouth kisses against the bared skin. Anxious to feel more, she struggled with the last few buttons as he tormented her, his hands lightly running from her neck down her back and up again. As the last button slid free, she shrugged the shirt off, and let it pool at her hips. Her skirt rode up as she shifted, wiggling to be closer to the heat of his body, needing to feel her breasts against his chest, her groin solidly locked against his.

Rick's muffled groan of masculine approval whispered over her skin, sending a fresh wave of heat to her pussy. She could feel her panties rapidly growing damp, the silky material pressing against her throbbing flesh. She wanted him inside of her, but he didn't seem to be in any hurry as his lips continued to leisurely sample her warm flesh, his fingertips softly stroking over her bared back.

Cupping her breasts in her hands, she unhooked the front clasp of her bra, baring her skin to the warmth radiating from his body. Rocking her hips, she surged against him, grinding her needy flesh against his erection. She knew he wanted her, his cock was straining against the denim of his jeans, but unlike her ex-husband, he wasn't making any move to unzip them and sink into her welcoming wetness.

Wanting to move things along, she reached between them, only to lose the feel of his touch against her skin as he grasped her wrists in his hands and pulled her hands away from his zipper. "Easy," he whispered against her neck, the warm of his lips sending a trail of fire along her nerve endings. She about screamed as he flicked his tongue against her pulse, then shifted back, unlocking her ankles from his waist with a roll of his hips. "Show me what you like."

Watching the way his gaze moved over her, she felt sexy. With Brian she wouldn't have been able to sit on the kitchen counter and touch herself. But there was something about the leashed intensity of Rick's eyes. The way he held himself still as she cupped a breast and rolled her nipple between the thumb and forefinger of one hand while her other hand slowly eased down her stomach to the top of her skirt, the way his breath caught as she shifted forward, braced the heels of her feet on the handles of her drawers and flipped her skirt up to bare her damp panties, emboldened her.

She wanted him to watch her, to see her as a sensual woman rather than his friend, needed him to desire her as she had him for so long. Sliding a hand inside her panties, she stroked it over her wet lips, barely daring to slip past.

"More." His voice was deeper than she had ever heard it, and it send a flutter of awareness throughout her body. She was going to make love with this man, was going to soon feel the slide of his hard length inside of her pussy, feel his cock surging in and out of her body.

Carefully, she lifted her hips and pushed her skirt and panties down, then kicked free of them. For a brief moment, she wondered what the hell she was doing sitting bare assed naked on her kitchen counter with Rick, but the flaring of his nostrils, the way he clenched his fists at his sides, pushed any fear aside. She wanted this, needed to be this woman with him, the kind of woman who knew what she wanted and went after it.

Still shy, she returned her hands to their earlier positions, and dipped her finger into her core, stroking it along her slick inner walls. A moan welled inside her and escaped at the feel of her fingernail lightly scraping her sensitive flesh. Rick groaned in echo and moved forward, his mouth slamming down over hers as his hands slid between them, his fingers joining hers in playing with her body.

Rick's lips burned down her neck, slowly moving lower, down her chest, her stomach, until he knelt down and pressed soft kisses against her inner thighs. Katherine's eyes almost crossed as he nipped at the tender skin.

Pulling her hands away, she moved them to her breasts, coating her nipples in her juices as she started pinching and pulling on them, sending sparks of pleasure-pain along her body to her clit.

Rick meandered his way to her pussy, his tongue lapping gently at her flesh and his fingers continued to play and torment her clit, holding her just on the edge of arousal, but not allowing her passions to build enough to drive her into orgasm.

Whimpering in need, she rocked her hips into his motions, trying to coax him into licking her where she needed it the most. Katherine could feel the moist heat of his breath brushing across her pussy, teasing her. When he showed no signs of cooperating, she decided to take control. Reaching down with one hand, she fisted it in his hair and tried to guide him where she wanted him. With Brian she never would have dared to do something so wanton. She had always let him set the pace, trusting him to take her with him, generally too swept up in the moment to give it much thought.

But with Rick she was aware of her body to a level she hadn't experienced before, and his leisurely pace allowed her to play, to explore to a deeper degree. He pulled his hands away from her pussy, spread her legs wider, and pressed his lips against her pussy-lips, a closed mouth kiss. Frustrated, she tried to push him away only to have him drive his tongue in fast and deep into her core while his fingers returned, pinching her clit and teasing along the seam of her lips. Squirming, she slid down on the counter until her hips hung over the edge and she could twist and recline, her body draped along the counter.

She could feel her orgasm quickly building. Returning her hands to her body, she caressed up and down her torso, stroking her body with the backs of her fingers, gliding them over her nipples and down along her sides. Rick settled into a steady thrusting with his fingers, lapping at her pussy with his tongue as his fingers retreated, while rolling her clit in tiny little circles with his thumb.

Sweet euphoria rushed over her within minutes, her core tightening around his tongue and fingers. With a gasp, she arched her back, tightened her body, and rode the wave as her orgasm rushed over her, her nerve endings exploding in unison.

She could feel Rick's tongue leave her, and was vaguely aware of him standing, but his fingers continued their magic, driving her quickly into a second orgasm, this one stronger than the first. Whispering his name softly, she pinched her nipples hard, increasing the sensations coursing through her.

She wasn't sure if she could stand, but she knew she wanted more, she wanted to feel his body covering hers. When his hands left body, she moaned softly in complaint.

"Shhh, Kath," he whispered as he slid his arms under, picking her up, and holding her against his bare chest. Katherine wrapped her arms around his neck, pressing soft kisses against his neck as he carried her down the hall.

"Which door?"

"Mmmm, the right," she managed to say against his neck. She didn't want to think any more, she just wanted to feel. She was tired of thinking. Closing her eyes, she drifted, held safe in his arms as he crossed her bedroom.

The next thing she was aware of was the cool feel of her sheets against her skin as he laid her down, then came down over her, his body a welcome weight. Clasping at his shoulders, she pulled him tight against her, her limber legs wrapping around his waist. Rubbing her damp pussy against the denim covering his crotch, she whimpered at the rough feel even as she increased the friction, her body demanding more.

"So much lost time," he whispered against her neck as his lips trailed a path of liquid heat, stinging her nerve endings. Her fluttered at his words, her throat tight with emotion.

"We have all the time in the world," she finally managed to whisper back as she slid her hands down his body, sliding them between their bodies to the button of his jeans. Nimbly working on the piece of metal, she managed to slide it free as he continued to kiss his way down her neck, along the curve of her collarbone and further downward until he was worshipping at her breasts. Working his zipper down, Katherine managed to open the fly enough so she could grasp Rick's cock, the smooth length hard and hot in her hands.

With a groan muffled against her breasts, Rick wiggled out of her grasp and knelt between her legs. Pushing his jeans down his hips he bared his cock fully to her gaze. Trailing her gaze over his body, she smiled lazily.

This was the man she had been waiting for forever.

As Rick slid off of the bed and stood, his hands quickly pushed his jeans and briefs from his body, she rolled over and fumbled in the nightstand drawer, pulling out a foil package. She ripped it open and had it ready when Rick knelt between her legs again.

Sitting up, she quickly rolled the latex sheath over his cock, then wrapped her arms around his neck and pulled him back into the welcoming heat of her body. His cock nudged at the entrance of her pussy, and she arched against him, craving the firm heat of him plunging deep inside of her, filling her.

Tipping her head up, she pressed her lips against his, claiming his mouth with her tongue as he rocked forward, his cock infinitely slow in joining them together. Whimpering into his mouth, she wrapped her legs around his waist and pulled him in tighter. Her pussy fluttered as his cock slid deeper, then retreated. She could feel the slap of his pelvis against hers as he thrust, his hips gliding up and down the sensitive skin of her inner thighs.

Breaking the kiss, she gasped out her pleasure, moans filling the room as he picked up the pace. Holding tight to his shoulders, she dug tiny crescents with her hails as he settled into a steady rhythm. Her body hummed with desire, every nerve ending screaming for more, for the sensations to never end.

Rick's breathing grew harsh as he dropped his head to lie next to hers on the pillow, his face pressed against the curve of her neck. Sliding her arms further around him, she stroked them over his back and down to his ass. Gripping the soft skin, she pressed him as tight into her body as she could with each down stroke.

Her body damp with their sweat, she was reaching for the stars, her slick inner muscles clutching at Rick's cock, growing tighter with each thrust. Until, with a soft scream, she climaxed, her moans echoing off the bedroom walls.

She was dimly aware of the tightness of his body, the faster, shorter strokes within her as he rushed toward his own orgasm, driving her back over the crest into yet another of her own. Holding him tight, she fought to recover her breath, needing to say so many things to him.

A while later, she opened her eyes and looked into Rick's twinkling blue ones, feeling satisfied emotionally as well as physically for the first time in a long while. Cupping his strong jaw in her hand Katherine rose up from where she rested against his chest and kissed him, needing to convey to him in some way what she was feeling, but unsure if either was ready for the words. As she pulled away, she curled back up against his chest, his hands stroking through her damp hair. "There's so much I feel like we should talk about. So much that needs to be said."

His hands stilled for a moment at her words, and her heart leaped, uncertain of what he would say. "I think there's a lot we should have said before now. But right now, in this moment, holding you in my arms, I am content to wait so long as you know that you mean more to me than just a friend. That I want more from you than that."

Katherine pressed a soft kiss against his breastbone, the sprinkle of hair on his chest tickling her nose. "So do I Rick. I always did."

* * *

MICHELLE HOUSTON

Willed to Love

A SECOND CHANCE AT LOVE

WILLED TO LOVE

Ashley leaned back in her chair and tipped her head, subtly wiping the tears that were welling in her eyes. As various family members filed into the room and claimed seats, she made sure not to meet anyone's eyes. She wasn't wanted, and she knew it. Nervous, she twisted the simple gold band on her ring finger, waiting until the lawyer decided to finally start telling everyone what they got in the will.

The chair next to her creaked when weight settled in to it, and a firm hand clasped over hers startling her. Looking up into her soon to be ex's warm eyes, she found herself unable to look away. Her heart ached with the need to collapse in his arms and cry out her pain. His paternal grandmother had been the only person in his family that had accepted her, had made her feel welcome. Now the grand lady was dead, and she was surrounded by hostility. She could only imagine what Devon's family was thinking, wondering why she present.

In fact, Ashley was having that same thought.

"She loved you, you know?"

Pinching her trembling lips together, Ashley nodded. The sympathy in Devon's voice was almost her undoing. He had lost his grandmother, and here he was trying to comfort her. How she loved him.

Glancing around the room though, she saw the curled lips and flared nostrils, the squinted eyes and the gazes that wouldn't make contact. His family hadn't changed their opinion of her, and she doubted they ever would.

Her inability to provide him with an heir was only one of the reasons. As the thought entered her mind, a flash of pain followed. Pulling her hand away, Ashley broke eye contact and curled into herself, the way she had had to after her pregnancy ended in miscarriage. Devon had been out of the country, and she had been alone, surrounded by people who didn't give a shit about her.

Two days she had lain in a hospital bed before someone thought to let his grandmother know what happened, and she had had to be the one to call him and let him know that she had miscarried.

"Well, since everyone is here, I guess we can get started." As the lawyer started pulling papers out of a briefcase, those that were milling around the room settled into available chairs and leaned against walls. Only the warmth coming from next to her where Devon sat kept her in her chair.

She didn't want to be there, but the lawyer had insisted that her presence was vital. But as he droned on, detailing the dozens upon dozens of bequeaths to various family members, Ashley was giving serious consideration to sneaking out when her name was called.

"And to my grandson Devon and granddaughter-in-law Ashley, I leave my house, the remainder of my trust-fund from my father, and a variety of jewelry and other personal items that are itemized, on the condition that they spend six months together in the house before perusing their divorce further. Should they decline, they both forfeit the right to anything from my estate. Should they agree, then all previous bequeaths to any member of the family are conditional upon their agreement to support Devon and his wife's attempted reconciliation. Any attempt to convince them not to reconcile, now or in the future, will be seen as an automatic forfeit of claim to any part of my estate, as well as an agreement to reimburse the estate for anything previously accepted."

Ashley almost giggled at the sudden silence. The old adage about a pin dropping came to mind, momentarily cutting through her grief. Devon's grandmother had been big on speaking her mind, using old age as her justification. It shouldn't have come as a surprise that her will reflected her personality.

"In addition, should Ashley agree to spend six months with Devon, an additional settlement for her, including property for an artist studio, has been arranged regardless of the outcome of their attempted reconciliation."

Ashley felt like a clamp had wrapped around her heart. Devon's grandmother knew all of her hot buttons, and just where to push to get what she wanted. But despite the incentive, Ashley didn't know if she would be able to do it. She still loved Devon with every fiber of her being, and the idea of spending six months 'working on their marriage' was enough to rip out her heart.

She desperately wanted to reconcile with him, but the same thing was holding her back each time--his family.

"What do you say Ash?"

Looking into his blue eyes, she wanted to scream yes. His firm lips, slightly parted, begged for her to kiss him. Her pulse raced remembering the last time they had made love, just months before. It had been the night before he left on his business trip.

She had stripped for him, shy about the changes to her body, emboldened by the desire she had seen in his eyes. His mouth and hands had worshipped her, caressing her curves and the slight budge of her belly. Her breasts responded to the memory and grew heavy. Sitting there at the reading of his grandmother's will and getting aroused wasn't her idea of a good time, but Devon had always had that effect on her. She could be doing almost anything, and he could get her pulse racing.

Ignoring everyone else in the room, she focused on him. According to how the will was worded, they would be complete idiots to interfere now, and Ashley knew his family to be anything but idiots. Many of them had gone to Ivy League colleges, and currently ran their own businesses, or were firmly planted in the area of politics.

Cold yes. Idiots? Not by a long shot.

"I know this means a lot to you Devon, since it is part of your inheritance. But do you really want to do this?"

Devon's eyes clouded with pain, and Ashley almost broke down herself.

"You're the one who walked out on me Ash, not the other way around. Remember?"

97

She remembered all too well. The painful decision to leave, despite how much she loved him. The atmosphere they had lived in was emotionally poisonous and he wasn't willing to just walk away. She had tried to make him see how much she hated living under his family's thumb. Losing the baby had been her breaking point.

So she had packed up and left him, taking only her cherished belongings.

And now the one person she had loved in his family was pushing her back into the situation, but with a twist. None of the family could reject her, or push Devon to leave her. She would be permitted as part of the family, even if not welcomed. But could she survive such a situation? Would her creativity, her passion for art, and her love for Devon survive?

"I am also instructed to give you this before you decide." Ashley glanced away from Devon to find the lawyer holding a sealed envelope out to her. Hands trembling, she reached for it, and had to read it three times before she could make sense of it. When she did, the enormity of the situation hit her like a cement truck.

Carefully she folded the letter and put it back into the envelope, then tucked it into her purse. Looking the lawyer in the eyes she told him, "I agree to the terms of the will."

"Very well then, here's the keys to the house and please, call on me if you have any questions. As for everyone else, that does it. There are a few more bequeaths, but they are for household staff, some of the charities Mrs. Monroe worked with, and so on. Nothing I am sure you wish to be bothered with."

Judging by the speed at which everyone left the room, the lawyer was right. Ashley also had a suspicion that no one else caught the irony in his tone either. Then again, a quick glance at Devon confirmed that he had gotten it. His lips were pressed so tightly together they were turning white. Not from anger though, judging by the faint shaking of his shoulder, but from trying not to laugh.

Excusing herself, Ashley stood and moved to the doorway, Devon fast on her heels.

"Ash, wait."

Keeping her back to him as she twisted her hands, holding herself together by sheer willpower, she told him she would be gathering her things and meet him at the house in a few days, where they would begin their six months together.

"I'll drive you."

"Devon, I--" Her voice cracked and she had to take a deep breath, then another, and another. His hand, so firm and gentle, settled on her shoulder, silently offering her comfort that she wasn't sure she could handle. She just wanted to get away from everyone and lick her wounds.

"I need some time. This is a lot to take in, and I just need some time alone."

"I--" Now it was his turn to pause and clear his throat. "I didn't ask Nana to do this, but I'm glad she did. I've missed you Ash."

They stood silently for a few moments before the warmth of his hand left her shoulder and she could hear the soft thud of his steps down the hallway, moving away from her. Forcing one foot in front of the other, she headed in the other direction, not stopping until she was in her car.

* * *

It only took her two days to gather her things and put most of her affairs in order for a six month leave. Her boss was pissed, to say the least, but given Devon's family's influence, he wasn't about to cause her any problems. So her leave was considered bereavement time, and they were leaving it at that.

As she pulled into the drive leading up to Mrs. Monroe's house, she couldn't help reflecting how she had come full circle. Almost six years before she had driven up this path for the first time. She had worked at a catering service at the time, and was part of the staff brought in for a fall party launching the political career of one of 'the grandchildren', as Devon's grandmother referred to them. Never by name, except Devon.

A few hours in, the old lady had cornered her and ordered her to keep her company. Her feet killing her, thanks to the high heels she had worn to counter her five foot five frame, Ashley had been more than grateful for the excuse to sit down for a while. It was while they had been discussing philosophy that Devon had gone looking for Nana, and found her sitting in the corner of her library giggling like a school girl with Ashley.

Sparks had flown, and not good ones either. Her heart raced just remembered facing him down, his six foot frame dwarfing her as he demanded to know what she wanted with his grandmother. Temper flaring, she had fired back that if he hadn't left his grandmother to seek companionship from strangers, he would have a better ability to watch over her.

As she pulled up to the house, she could almost hear Devon's voice suddenly changing from confrontation to admiration, and then he had asked her out. Of course she had turned him down, which had started their whirlwind courtship that finally cumulated with their marriage a year later.

A little over six months later, she had wanted out. Not out of Devon's life, but out of the cycle his family had fallen in to. She had spent every waking moment being groomed to be a socially acceptable wife, and failed on all counts. She laughed too loud. She cried in public. She wore clothing with too much color and not enough style. She actually dared to laugh in a senator's face. All sins in the Monroe's eyes.

Feeling her whole body trembling, Ashley climbed out of the car and gently closed the door. She desperately wanted to jump back into the car, slam the door behind her and peel rubber all the way back down the driveway; because she had just noticed Devon standing in the shadows, watching her. Running a hand through her riot of curls, she tried to tame her red locks without much success as she walked across the drive and up the stairs.

As she reached the porch, uncertainly clawed at her. What should she do? He was still her husband, but they had been waiting out the separation requirements until they could file for divorce. Two months they hadn't spoken to each other, except through lawyers and his grandmother. Yet the love was still there, as was the almost insatiable desire that arched between them.

"Hello Ash." As he held out his hand, she had no choice but to clasp it. Her heart demanded that she not do anything further to hurt him, but her head reminded her that she couldn't live the life his family demanded of her. Although, she did have hope that his grandmother's will had changed some things, there were some members of the family wealthy enough that they could shrug off the restrictions and do as they damn well pleased.

For some, it wouldn't matter either way, wealth or not. She wasn't of their class, and they weren't about to accept her. Ironically, it was the wives that were the most judgmental. Devon's brothers, uncles and cousins seemed to treat her with a casual indifference.

As her hand slid into his warm one, he used it to pull her close and wrapped her in his arms. Sinking into his embrace, she allowed herself to close her eyes and just feel for a moment; the heat of his body, the beat of his heart, the rush of need and desire, the feeling of being loved and protected. She wrapped her arms around his neck and just held on, as he held her close, his hands warm against her hips.

The loss of his grandmother was killing her slowly. She had cried herself to sleep the last two nights, and knew she probably would again tonight. Despite their age different, Nana had come to be a good friend, someone she could always turn to, even if she couldn't bring herself to do so.

Curled in his arms, she could almost forget the events of the last few months. The first few days of conversations with Devon, as she tried to get him to understand that she couldn't be the wife he was expected to have. Finally, her heart threatening to rip apart, she had uttered the D word, and the next thing she knew, lawyers were involved and everything was spiraling out of control.

She had wanted a separation, some time to heal and think. Instead, his family had jumped on her simple question--*did Devon want out?*--and run with it. Now, standing there in his arms, she had hopes that they could work things out. But she was realistic enough to know it would take time, for both of them.

All too soon, she forced herself to pull away and forced herself to look him in the eyes. "Well, I guess we need to get me a room picked out."

Devon's eyed hardened with determination, and she had a feeling she wouldn't like what was coming. "Nana's will stipulated that we actively work on reconciliation. Separate rooms, and ignoring each other for six months isn't going to cut it Ash. You're sleeping in the room with me. Now if you don't like the one I have picked out, you are welcome to have our things moved to another bedroom. But we are staying together."

Nope, she didn't like it at all. But remembering the letter from his grandmother tempered her tongue and she managed to just nod. Damn the old meddling woman. She knew just where to pull and push to get her way.

* * *

Ashley's first evening in the house was outside of anything she had expected. Rather than treat her as an interloper, Nana's staff welcomed her, and even pampered her. Some she remembered from the few days of her visits with Devon's grandmother. The old butler, Bernard, was a particular favorite of hers. She never would have guessed it to look at him, but the white haired gentleman's gentleman was just that. And he could gossip and giggle with the best of them.

With a sigh, she leaned back against the chair in the library and closed her eyes, just letting the peace of the house soak into her pores.

"Oh come now my dear, surely you can do better than that."

Ashley's eyes flared open, only to find herself still alone in the room. She would have sworn she had heard the lingering echo of Lillian's laughter in the room. Wiping away a tear, she closed her eyes again, relaxed and just let herself remember.

"Oh come now my dear, surely you can do better than that. It's been so long since I've had any decent girl talk." Looking at Lillian, Ashley couldn't imagine the dignified lady ever discussing such things as sex and orgasms, but that was exactly what she was aiming for.

"I'm not asking for the dirty details dear girl, but just answer me this. Does my grandson measure up to past experiences?"

Having taken a sip of her tea to try and gather her thoughts, Ashley wound up spitting it out. And in Lillian's direction. Almost immediately, the every attentive shadow in the room, dashed to her side with a white handkerchief.

"Here we are now Ms. Ashley."

"Thank you Bernard," she responded, shocked that she had actually forgot that he was in the room.

"Oh do quit hovering Bernard and sit down. You're welcome to join in the conversation, but you have to dish out your fair share as well. Just remember, I know you've been sneaking out at night to spend time was that new gardner, what's his name?"

"Adam, Ms. Lillian."

"Ah yes, Adam. Now there is a fine looking young man." As Devon's grandmother smiled her dreamy smile, Ashley breathed a mental sigh of relief. *Maybe she was going to get out of here today without spilling what Lillian wanted to hear most – how Devon had managed to get her into 'the sack'.*

She must have made some sign of relief though, because Lillian's gaze turned to her. "Don't worry dear, I haven't forgotten about you. So tell, how did Devon manage to convince you to bed him?"

Lost in her memories, she didn't hear the door open. The first sign she was not longer alone was the warmth of Devon's hands on her shoulders. "Ashley honey? Dinner's done."

Opening her eyes, she looked into his gaze, into eyes the mirror of his grandmother's, and burst into tears. Within moments, she found herself curled up in his lap, the front of his shirt soaked with her tears, and balling like a newborn baby.

Soothing and patient, his hands ran over her back, smoothed her hair down, and he simply held her as she mourned.

* * *

Ashley stood at the window looking out over the dreary day, feeling much like the weather outside. Ever since she had allowed her grief to overwhelm her, she had worked twice as hard to keep it contained. Lillian would have wanted her to move on, to remember the good times, but she was finding it harder to not dwell.

First the baby, then her husband, and now the woman who was arguably her best friend. If things didn't work out with Devon this time, she wasn't certain she would survive it.

She smelled Devon before she saw him, the faint yet heady scent of his cologne. Warm hands settled on her hips, and slowly Devon pressed against her back, his arms wrapping around her waist. His chin came to rest on the top of her head, and in the silence, she could hear her heart pick up its pace.

Almost dreamily, she relaxed back against him, the familiarity of the pose offering a strange comfort to a world gone mad with grief.

She wasn't sure how long they stood there, watching the rain fall, before the temperature in the room spiked. Devon pressed soft lips against her neck, and unconsciously Ashley closed her eyes and relaxed into the touch. She craved this, in a way she had never been able to deny. Devon had always known just where to touch, and he had never left her wanting while fulfilling himself.

Unable to handle the pain of reality, she let herself get lost in the moment, accepting the comfort he offered. As his hands slid up on her ribs, and cupped her breast through the thin T-shirt she was wearing, Ashley's pussy clenched. Her body was coming awake after a long slumber.

Trembling at the surge of sensations that threatened to drown her, she tipped her head back and met Devon's lips. It was only a brief brush of lips, but it renewed the demands of her body. Slowly, Devon's hands stroked back down her body, coming to rest on her stomach.

Like a cold splash of water, it woke Ashley to the here-and-now. Almost franticly, she pulled away and crossed the room. Panting at the pain that threatened to send her to her knees, she looked into Devon's stricken eyes.

"Ash?" He reached out his hand, but Ashley shook him off. Pressing her hands to her stomach, she could almost feel the echo of his touch, her skin still heated from his hands. Under her hands, where her baby should have rested, she felt empty.

"Baby, talk to me."

"I can't Devon. I can't do this. Not yet."

Running a hand through his hair, Devon paced across the room, agitation obvious with each step. As he paced back, she could see by the pinch of his lips that she wasn't going to like what he had to say, but that he had bit his tongue as long as he was going to.

"Do you think it was easy for me? Finding out that you lost the baby and not a damn member of my family cared enough to call me, until Nana found out what was going on? Do you think it didn't rip me in fucking two to lose first the baby, and then you? To know that you were all alone in the hospital for two days!

You're not the only damn person hurting here Ash. I know you're in pain, I know you're confused and feeling lost and alone. But damnit, so am I. That was my baby too. I lost my baby, and then my wife!"

Before she had a chance to respond, Devon turned on his heel and stormed out of the room, the door whispering closed behind him.

* * *

Almost a week later, Ashley was sitting on the bed, brushing her hair when Devon came into the room. With a quick glance at her watch, she saw that he was about an hour earlier that normal. Despite his grandmother's death and their attempt at reconciliation, he had to work. His duties had actually increased, now that he was taking care of some of his grandmother's investments, and clearing up financial matters.

Most of Lillian's shares in companies, and responsibilities had gone to other family members. But her pet projects she had left to Devon. It was actually a blessing that she had. Otherwise, Ashley feared that Devon would have clung to her side, so worried about her and her sense of loss that he would have smothered her.

Part of it, she knew, was due to the loss of their baby. Having been out of the country, he knew some of the agony she had suffered alone.

With purposeful strides he crossed the room and leaned down, pressing a firm kiss against her lips. Startled, she found herself responding before she even knew what hit her. Devon had been affectionate over the last few days, holding her hand and touching her shoulder, even pulling her close for a hug. But not since her first night, had he kissed her, and then it had only been a soft press of his lips against her forehead as he held her.

As his tongue swept into her mouth, his hand cupped the back of her head, holding her still for his sensual assault. Breathless and lightheaded, Ashley opened her mouth further and allowed his tongue to rub against hers, to thrust into her mouth in a parody of what her body was craving. As the realization that her core was growing damp in preparation for his cock, she broke the kiss.

"Wha--?" She couldn't manage to put her thoughts to words. Why had he done that? They had been taking things slow, and now this.

Devon's hand relaxed in her hair, and gently he slid it down the side of her face until he cupped her cheek. Holding her still, he pressed a soft closed-mouth kiss against her lips then straightened.

"You just looked so beautiful sitting there that I couldn't resist."

Ashley pressed the fingertips of one hand against her lips as he turned away and headed into the bathroom, discarding his shirt and shoes along the way. As the shower turned on, she traced the pouting fullness of her well-kissed mouth.

"At least tell me this then. Can my grandson kiss?"

Lillian's laughter filled the room as Ashley felt her face heat with a blush. Beside her, Bernard did his best not to chuckle and soon lost. "I, well, that is. Lillian! Really, this isn't at all proper."

Flustered beyond anything she could remember, Ashley tried to figure out how to get herself out of this mess. First Devon's grandmother wanted to know about the sex life, and not getting the goods, she had settled on a tamer topic. But still it was one Ashley's didn't think appropriate to discuss with her boyfriend's grandmother. The beloved matriarch of the family.

"Just answer her sweetie. It's doesn't get any better if you try and ignore it." Glancing into Bernard's knowing eyes, Ashley gave up and with a nervous giggle whispered, "Yes, he does know how to kiss."

"I knew it!" Lillian clapped her hands together in glee. "At least one of the grandchildren has got it. Thankfully, it's Devon." Her joy transformed Lillian's face, until she lost some of the aged look the years and many disappointments had put on her, and Ashley could see some of the young woman that was buried, but not forgotten, coming to life.

"So really dear girl, sure you don't want to dish the dirt on your first night together?" The innocent look in Devon's grandmother's eyes should have clued her in. "I really would love to hear about it. It's been so long since I have felt the touch of a man, that I find I can almost remember what goes where if I think really hard about it."

Horrified at Lillian's words, and stunned at the droll tone she delivered them in, Ashley collapsed against Bernard's shoulder, surrendering to her laughter.

The shower shut off and Ashley pulled herself from the past and continued brushing her hair, trying to tame the wayward locks.

As Devon came back into the room, naught but a towel wrapped around his waist, she wanted to throw the hairbrush at him. Restraining the urge, more because it was an antique silver ivory handled brush that Lillian had given her, rather than because she didn't want to leave a bruise on his tanned, toned body.

Without making a sound, she climbed to her feet and calmly left the room, as if the sight of his bare chest and legs wasn't slowly turning her into a quivering mass of need.

* * *

Ashley hesitantly opened the door to Nana's bedroom a few days later, her heart aching as she was enveloped in the light floral scent the lady favored. As she stepped into the room, she could almost see Lillian propped up on her bed, a dozen pillows all around her as she watched her guilty pleasure – daytime soaps. She had spent hours laying across the foot of the bed, munching on whatever delicious snacks Nana had ordered for the day, talking to the wise woman while watching TV with her.

They had had some of their best girl talks. More heart-to-hearts than anywhere else in the house, as if they had both reached an unspoken agreement to keep things completely serious while together alone in Lillian's bedroom. It wasn't a place for gossip, or for teasing. It was just the two of them alone, best friends. Crossing the room, Ashley flopped down on her back and the bed, tears shimmering in her eyes.

"Oh Lillian, what am I going to do?"

Turning on her side, she curled up on the comforted, pulling at partially around her as she poured out her pain to the one woman who she knew would understand.

"I love him so much! But god, it hurts. Looking into his eyes, wanting him so badly I shake with it, and then the pain returns. I died a little inside when we lost the baby, and I know he is going to eventually want another one. But what if I can't carry to term?" Under the warmth of the comforter, Ashley pressed her hands tight against her stomach and gave her tears free reign.

Sometime later, she woke to firm hands lifting her. Only partially awake, she curled against Devon's chest, trusting him not to drop her as he carried her down the hall to their bedroom. With a sleepy smile, she pressed a soft kiss against his jaw.

Wrapping her arms around his neck, she snuggled close, murmuring a protest when he put her down on the bed and moved to pull away. Tightening her hold, she pulled him down with her, until his familiar weight settled against her body. Without opening her eyes, she ran her heads down his chest, stroking over the muscles he had had to work hard to attain. With so much of his life spent behind a desk, he had always taken an hour four times a week to hit the gym, something she had grown to very much appreciate. Especially once they got a home gym set, and she could watch him work out, the sweat dripping from his body.

His hands stoked over her back, and when Ashley moved to pull him over her, he held her still and whispered softly in her ear. She vaguely heard his words; soft apologies, love words, the outpouring of his pain. Emotionally exhausted, she laid in the circle of his arms, held safe and loved, and drifted back to sleep.

* * *

Several days later, Ashley was still trying to settle into some semblance of a routine. Devon made sure that the staff knew not to disturb her when she was in the room he had designated as her studio. All of her canvases and paints had been brought from her apartment and set up in what had once been a sitting room. She could remember sitting there for hours, spending time with Devon's grandmother, listening to stories about him as a child. If they weren't in the library or her bedroom, then they were in here.

The only savings grace was that his family had left them alone, so far none daring to challenge the family matriarch's wishes.

In the evenings, they had fallen into the patterns of sharing dinner together and then retired to their suite, where Devon worked on paperwork and she read, watched TV or tried to ignore the way her body was demanding a response to her husband. Most evenings they sat around and talked, often about nothing in particular. Neither of them broached the subject they most needed to work past, the miscarriage and why she had walked out. He knew some of what had happened, but she hadn't been able to tell him everything. And now, she wasn't certain that she could relive it all again to tell him.

Their time in the evenings was almost like a memory, a dream of what it had been like on their honeymoon, minus the intense sex. Devon hadn't tried to go beyond a few kisses since the day he had found her sleeping on his grandmother's bed, and none had been as passionate as before that day. And as the days passed, she waited, uncertain how to approach the subject of a true reconciliation, uncertain if she was ready to pick things up where they had left off. Although she had been half asleep, she still remembered the things he had said, the pain that had laced every word.

She knew he wanted things the way they were. So it should have been easy to say "I don't want a divorce. I want you." But time after time she tried, and each time, the words got stuck. How could they go back to how they were, as if their baby had never happened? How could they bridge the pain that still separated them?

Her heart still ached, and some times, she found herself rubbing a hand over her belly before she remembered that the baby was gone. Sometimes, she'd look up and find Devon's eyes on her, and the urge to curl up in his arms and cry was so strong, she almost broke down.

At night, she always turned in first, determined to be asleep before he came to bed, but in the morning she woke with her body tangled with his. It was damned frustrating, and she was about to strangle the love of her life if he didn't stop the subtle war he was waging. She wasn't ready yet.

She made sure not to walk about unclothed, always covering up her body and wearing the simplest and most unflattering night clothes. Devon on the other hand would walk out of the shower with a towel around his waist, another around his shoulders, and nothing else. They both knew what he was doing, and he was winning. Foolishly, she had shown him that it got to her, seeing him like that, and he was using it to his advantage.

They had always been affectionate with each other, making love most every night. Over time they had expected the intensity to abate, but rather than cool it matured, until they could take their time with each other, to take things slow and leisurely explore rather than race to the finish line.

The last couple weeks though, it had felt like her libido had flashed back to the past, and was showing no signs of a return to the status quo.

Her showers had been getting longer and longer as she took care of her body's needs, like she was currently doing. Just a few minutes before, Devon had been in the shower, and she could picture how he had looked, the water sliding over his tanned body, down his firm stomach to his groin where the droplets caressed his hard cock.

The same hard cock she was wishing was buried in side of her, rather than her fingers.

And his ass, oh man his ass, with the drops of water rolling down it, covering the backs of his legs as it headed to his feet. Her hands itched to cup his ass as he surged into her, burying his cock deep and hard within her pussy.

Leaning back against the shower wall, she tried to assuage the burning need within her, but for the first night in several long and lonely months, an orgasm was denied her. Frustrated, she removed her hand from between her legs and slapped it against the tile. She could hear Devon moving around in the bedroom, opening drawers and generally making noise. Every night before, she had managed to get in her shower while he was still finishing up paperwork, but tonight he had beat her to it.

Her nightly shower was the only way she had been able to take the time to readjust to him without rushing into a return to their sexual lives. She needed the time.

Closing her eyes, she tried to work herself back to the fever pitch by rolling her nipples around and using the removable showerhead between her legs. She was almost to the point of release when a rush of cool air entered the room, followed by Devon's voice. "Ash? You ok in there?"

Her eyes flared open and she dropped the showerhead as she hurried to turn her back to the room, hoping her husband hadn't seen what she was doing. The showerhead clattered the to tile floor, bringing Devon into the room even as she responded, "I'm fine."

"You sure? You've been in here a while, and I got worried."

Glancing at him over her shoulder, Ashley saw the frank approval in his gaze as it trailed over her body. Almost flauntingly, she turned to face him. Her body flared to life, egged on by frustrated needs, her nipples hardened as he watched with a faint glint in his eyes that she knew so well.

As she watched the towel he was still wearing around his waist fluttered to the floor, leaving him gloriously naked. She couldn't bring herself to say anything as he moved into the bathroom, opened the shower door and stepped inside.

Instant explosions went off within her as he pulled her against him and kissed her, months of frustrated passion, of hopeless need cresting, threatening to sweep them both away. Weak-kneed, she wrapped her arms around his neck and let him pulled her tight against his body, the warm water cascading down them as he lifted her, fitting her into the curves of his larger frame, supporting her slighter weight on his hands.

"Damn baby I love you," he whispered as he pressed kisses against her cheek and down her neck. "I missed you so much."

Tears spilled from Ashley's eyes as she tipped her head back, silently consenting to whatever happened. It had been weeks in the making, and thanks to his grandmother's letter, which she had read multiple times a day since she had agreed to the reconciliation, she was ready to give them a second chance. She had to.

Every day she had been apart from him had been lonely, and she had almost gone back several times. Only the faint stretch marks on her stomach, the baby clothes locked away in a hope chest, and memory of mocking laughter at her darkest moments held her back. She hadn't been strong enough to face the rejection of his family again. Hadn't been strong enough to tell him everything that had happened.

But Devon's Nana had changed everything with the letter she had left as the last of her legacy.

Dearest Ashley,

I gave up a lot in my life. Nothing I regretted more however than the love of my life. My family didn't approve of him, you see. They had other plans for me.

And so I have spent most of my life alone, surrounded by a family that I grew to resent just as much as I hated the man my family forced me to marry.

Devon has been the only bright light in my life; the child of my eldest, who was taken from me too soon. He is my legacy.

Don't walk away from him. Fight for him, as I didn't fight for my beloved. Screw the rest of the family. I've done all I can to protect you from them, and from the secret that you need to hold close to your heart. For you see, I didn't tell anyone, although I suspect my husband knew, that I was pregnant when I married him.

His father was brought to life out of love, and that love continues on in Devon.

Loosing Devon's dad a few years back was almost as hard on me as when I had to walk away from his father. When your baby died, and you left, the sun stopped shining for two of us – Devon and myself. He deserves more than he will ever find with his kin, and he is coming to realize that.

I don't know what all passed between you and my children, but it if is true to their form, it was hellish and completely unfair. Blame them, hate them. But don't punish Devon, and yourself.

Remember dear, now you can tell the family to go to hell, and they can't do a thing about it. Saving face is important to them, but money is at the heart of all that they do. My husband taught them well. I hope that my passing gives you the means to rekindle what was once there, and save what I lost.

All my love, and greatest affection,
Lillian

Wrapping her legs around her husband's waist, she arched against him as his lips trailed down to her breasts. "I love you too," she gasped as his cock rubbed against the cleft of her body, teasing her with what was to come.

Gently, as he always had, he lifted her up, his moist nether lips pressed against his stomach, her breasts dangling in front of his face. As if he had all the time in the world, he stroked his tongue over one of her nipples. Nipping at it lightly with his teeth, he tugged just enough to draw a gasp of pleasure-pain from her before turning his attention to the other nipple.

Lavishing equal attention between her two nipples, he alternated back and forth, curling his tongue around the hardened bud and nipping at it with his strong teeth.

Ashley clutched at his shoulders, her nails digging into the tanned flesh as her body demanded more. She wanted him to fill her, to make her feel whole again as she hadn't felt since she left him. Her body ached in memory of what it was like to have his cock push deep into her pussy, stretching her until she thought she would scream from the sweet sensations.

Breathless, she started begging, "Devon, please!" hoping he would finally join them together. Thankfully, he understood and brought her back down his body, his cock nudging at her outer lips, then slipping partway into her core. Trembling at the flush of sensations, Ashley wiggled in his arms, eager to deepen their contact.

"I can't go through this again. Whatever happens, we work through it together."

Ashley's eyes flared open and she looked into his blue ones, startled to find tears shimmering in their depths. "Yes," she agreed, heartbroken that she had hurt him so badly, "I promise we will." At the time, it had seemed the only way. Now she knew she should have trusted him to help her, trusted him to choose her, to love her enough.

He jerked his hips and fully seated himself within her, then pressed her back against the cool, moist tile and started thrusting. Still holding his shoulders, Ashley loosened her body, riding the flow of his motions. Each thrust delivered the sweetest sensations as his cock slid against her slick inner muscles, the friction sending a riot of impulses through her nervous system.

Tipping her head back, she arched against him, her body quickly building to its peak, thanks to her frustrated earlier efforts at an orgasm. Devon pressed tight against her, his breathing harsh in her ear as he pumped his hips, working his cock deep and dark into her, then pulling back just enough to surge in again.

Ashley could feel her body tightening, her orgasm fast threatening to claim her. She wrapped her arms around his neck and started whispering in his ear, telling him how good he made her feel, describing the sensations coursing throughout her body. Begging him to fuck her harder.

That was one thing she hadn't been willing to change, no matter what. Devon loved it when she talked dirty, and even when she was dressing differently, eating differently, and trying her best to fit in, she refused to listen to the wives advice about her sexual relationship with her husband. How she should encourage him to seek his pleasure elsewhere while she worked to create the perfect home for him, the perfect foil for his entry into politics. Something Devon had been adamant her didn't want, on both counts.

"You burn me up baby, fucking scorch me right to the bone." Ashley thrilled at his gravely tone as he reciprocated, not as eloquent, but certainly as turned on.

Dropping one hand from his shoulders to slide between them, she started rubbing and plucking her clit, sending shivers down her spine and tremors through her pussy. Gasping as Devon shifted his angle, she couldn't hold back any longer. Her body clenching around him, she came, milking his cock with her inner muscles as he shortened his strokes and started pumping faster.

Her back slapped against the tile wall with each motion. Moments later, Devon groaned in her ear and his hips stopped rocking. She could feel the flow of his come deep in her core. She wanted to drop to her knees and suck the rest out of him, tasting the tang of her juices on his cock as he filled her mouth, but months without his vigorous lovemaking had feeling sore, and tired already.

She doubted she would even be able to stand upright when he let her go. Thankfully, she didn't have to. He somehow managed to get the taps turned off and out of shower and into the bedroom, with a towel, without disturbing her.

Still wrapped tightly around him, Ashley trilled inside as he dropped the towel over a chair and settled into it, his softening cock still slightly inside of her. As he leaned back and shifted hr position, so that she straddled him, and yet curled against his chest, she could feel his pussy begging for her. Her clit was hard and swollen, still tingling from her last orgasm.

In tune with her body, despite their absence from each other, Devon slid a hand between them and with a gentle touch, swirled his fingertip over her clit. It was just enough to reawaken the slumbering need inside of her. Rocking against his cock, Ashley closed her eyes and leaned her head against his shoulder, and let her husband coax another orgasm out of her worn out body.

As the last traces left her, she lifted her leg up and over and repositioned herself so that she lay curled up in his lap, still deliciously naked.

Devon stroked his hands up and down her back, and over her arms, as they cuddled together. An eternity passed, before his deep voice disturbed the silence. "I love you," he whispered, a slight catch to his voice as he spoken.

"I love you too."

* * *

Almost six months after Nan's death, Ashley was ready to wash her hands of the whole situation and dump everything in Devon's lap. Against her better judgment, she had decided to invite his family over for a small, intimate dinner, where they would announce their formal reconciliation now that the period asked for in the will was drawing to an end. The lawyers had already been called off, and Ashley wanted nothing more than to savor having Devon back in her life. But she had felt that his family, cold and cruel that they were, deserved more than an email. Which was how Devon had originally planned to tell them.

She had debated phoning them, but decided she didn't want to give them the opportunity to hang up on her. It was Bernard who had come to the rescue, and suggested a simple family dinner, with one addition.

After an hour with his family, she was ready to get up and walk out, after telling them all to get the hell out. The only thing holding her back was the presence of Nana's lawyer, who Bernard has suggested inviting. He sat midway down the table, a small smile curling his lips.

Ashley found herself thankful he had accepted the invitation, after for the thousandth time one of the aunts looked at her, opened her mouth to say something, glanced at the lawyer and turned her attention back to her dinner.

As Devon stood and struck his water glass with his fork, the conversation around the table fell silent. Looking into her husband's warm gaze, Ashley shifted in her seat, nervous about the reaction that were about to get.

"As you all now know, Ashley and I are officially back together, and I want to thank you all for giving us time to work things out between us." Droll though his tone was, not a hint of sarcasm dripped from his words. He had that in common with his grandmother; both of them had been able to deliver the sarcastic and the humorous, without batting an eye or their voices betraying them.

'Not that they had much choice.' It was close, but Ashley managed not to say it. Darting a glance at Nan's lawyer, she saw by his face he was thinking the same thing. But if Devon could resist resorting to snide comments, so could she.

"Our reconciliation isn't the only reason we asked you all here tonight. We also wanted you to know that soon, we will have a new addition to our family. Ashley found out just the other day that she is pregnant."

Murmurs filled the room as Devon's family reacted to the news that she was again going to desecrate their illustrious gene pool. Rubbing a hand over her still flat stomach, Ashley fought against the tears that threatened to spill. She wasn't going to let Devon's family upset her. She wasn't going to do anything to risk her child's life.

"I know that previously, you didn't take well to our expecting a child, and were even worse when Ashley miscarried. Rather than embrace my wife, you humiliated her, shunned her, and worse, tormented her in her greatest hour of need. For that, I want you to know that this will be the last time you will ever be welcome in this house again.

Several gasps of outrage resulted, but thankfully not protests. The will was ironclad. Devon's grandmother had wanted them to have her home, the house that belonged to her family, not the Monroe's.

"The best part though, is that after today, you will also not be expected to socialize with either one of us again. See, shortly before Nana died, she made a confession to me, and since my father isn't alive to suffer for it, I see no reason not to share.

"While we share blood through Nana, I am not now, nor have I ever been a Monroe. My father was Nana's child through her first and only love, and Ashley and I have already started the process to have our last name changed to his. Soon we will be Mr. and Mrs. Devon Wallace. And you, my dear family, can kiss my ass."

Without waiting for any response, Devon held out his hand to Ashley, and together they left the room. As the door closed behind them, she could hear some of the wives screeching like wet hens, and the husbands trying vainly to calm them down before they said something that would nullify any part of Devon's grandmother's will. Calm and steady, Bernard was seeing to them, ushering them out of the house.

Ashley hated that it had come down to this, but Devon had made the decision after she had finally admitted what had happened during the days between the miscarriage and when she had packed up and left. Not wanting to dwell on it, she had simply asked not to be forced to attend functions with his family.

He had done her one step better.

As they entered their bedroom, safe in the knowledge that the butler was following their earlier directions to see his family out, Ashley wrapped her arms around Devon's waist and hugged him. Closing her eyes, she breathed in the heady fragrance that was cologne mixed with a scent that was all her husband.

"I knew the night I met you, when you defended Nana, that you were destined for me. I was a fool to let you go Ash."

Ashley held on tight to his chest, listening to the steady beat of his heart. "I knew it too, it just took a letter from a meddling lady to get it to sink in. Which brings up something I wanted to talk to you about. If we have a girl, I'd like to call her Lillian, after your Nana."

Devon tipped her chin up, and leaned down to press a soft kiss against her lips. "I'd like that, very much."

As Devon swept her into his arms and carried her to their bed, Ashley's gaze caught on the letter that was sitting on her nightstand. The lawyer had given it to her a few days before, when she and Devon had visited to fill out paperwork for a name chance, and to inform him of the status of their marriage.

Ashley,

Darling, you don't know how happy I am that this was the letter you received. I admit, I wrote another one, just in case things didn't go so well. I meddled, like I always do. But that is neither here, nor there, since you are reading this letter.

Know that I am smiling down on you, as you and Devon begin your lives together again. Regardless of what the road ahead may throw into your path, hold tight to my grandson, and you will make it through.

I love you both, my darlings. And I wish you all the love and happiness in the world.

I do wish dear girl that you had been more forthcoming with sharing during our girl talks, but I understand your reluctance. When someone doesn't matter to you, it's easy to tell about your sexual exploits. But when it's love, ah, when it's love my child, you want to hold the memories tight to your chest, so as not to tarnish them.

I knew that day in the library, when you were so reluctant to share even details of a kiss, that you were the one for my grandson. After all, I still wouldn't be willing to share details of my time with Devon's grandfather beyond that it was glorious, and filled with love and passion. As I wish your life to be.

Always and affectionately yours,
Lillian

* * *

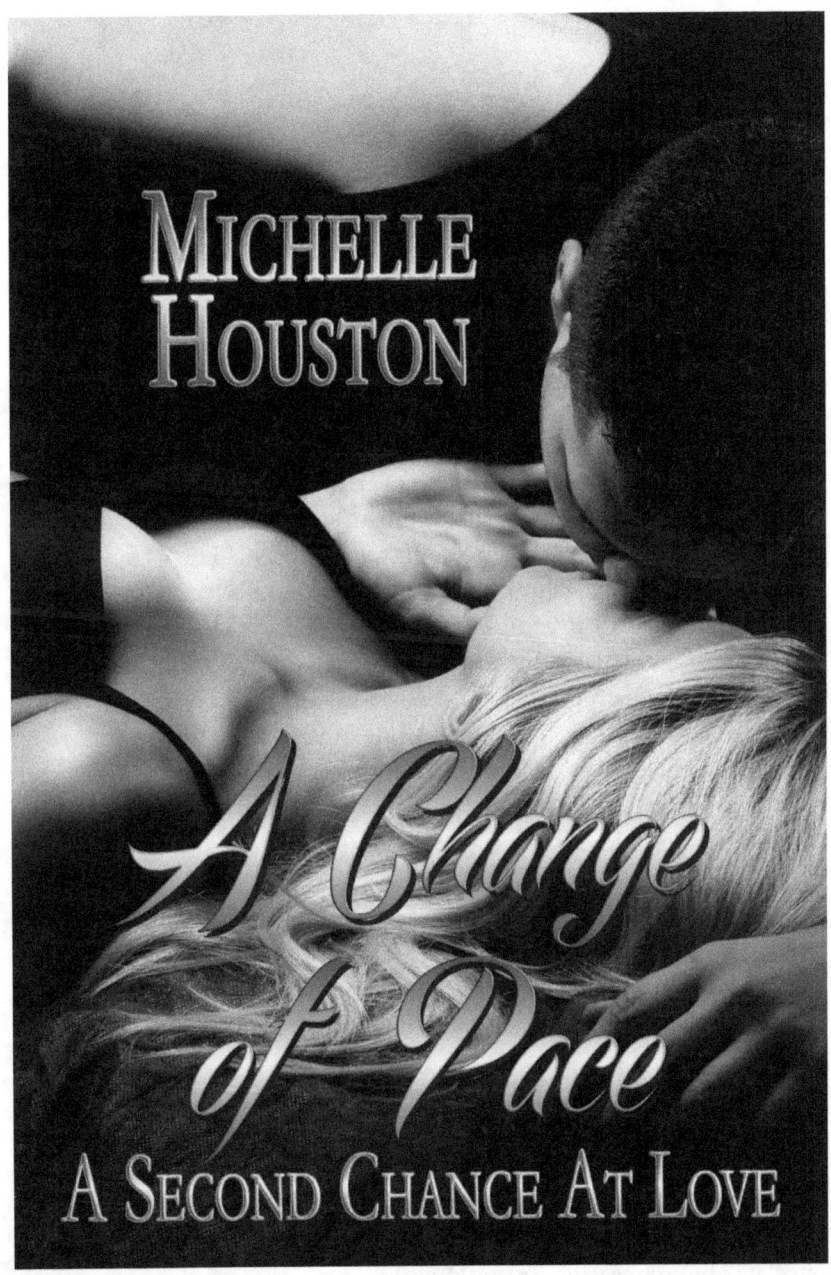

MICHELLE
HOUSTON

A Change
of Pace

A SECOND CHANCE AT LOVE

A CHANGE OF PACE

Nicole leaned back in her chair, debating whether she should knock off for the night or get a head start on next week's work. Looking out of the glass enclosure surrounding her office, at the already empty cubicles and the cleaning crew that was just arriving, she decided to call it a night. As if her body added its agreement she yawned, automatically covering her mouth with her hand.

Giving a mirthless laugh, she stood and packed up her things. Setting her computer to secure mode, she placed her keyboard in her desk drawer and locked it. Pulling her purse from the bottom drawer of the filing cabinet, she headed out of her office. There was no point in locking it—the cleaning crew had to get in to do their job.

As she walked down the lonely path to the elevator, she couldn't help sighing at what awaited her at home. A few plants that needed watering, a pile of laundry she needed to drop off at the cleaners, and a stack of bills to be paid. The weekend loomed ahead, empty.

Running a hand through her graying hair, she wondered for the thousandth time if this was the life she wanted. Ten years ago, fresh from college and idealistic as hell, she thought she could make a difference. She would start dating and maybe settle down in a year or so, when her career was steady, and hopefully a year or two later have her one and only child.

Now, here it was, ten years later, and she didn't even have a pet. Long hours at the office would leave it cooped up and alone inside her home. She didn't believe in doing that to a living creature. She had tried a fish, and ended up killing it when she kept forgetting to feed it. Even buying a supply of the vacation feeding pellets hadn't worked on the replacement fish. It had lasted only a month longer.

As she reached the elevator, she pushed the down button and waited. And waited. And waited.

"Elevator's out!" a helpful voice called out behind her. Groaning at the six-flight hike in high heels that awaited, she moved to the stairs and opened the door. Stepping into the stairwell, she was immediately enclosed in near darkness. Slipping off her shoes, she held them in one hand and gripped the rail in the other. Starting out slowly, she headed downstairs, grumbling with each step as the cold slowly seeped into her skin.

Rather than the prosecutor's office she had planned on joining out of college, student loans had forced her to accept an offer from an estate firm that had recruited her right out of law school. She had planned to stay just long enough to pay off her debt but had wound up buying a house, and now she found herself alone, thirty-five years old, with a mortgage that would take at least another twenty years to clear. In the darkness of the stairwell, she admitted to herself she hated her job. Writing wills and dealing with probates wasn't what she had planned on doing, or even imagined, when she graduated. But it was too late to start over.

Feet aching, she finally reached the ground floor and, before stepping out, she put her shoes back on, then moved out of the darkness. Waving to the security guard, she was buzzed out.

The muggy night air had her feeling sweaty and more irritated before she made it halfway to her car. Fed up with it all, she decided she wasn't ready to head home to the silence that would surround her, slowly suffocating her until she gave up and called it a night.

As she climbed into her car, she decided to head to a nearby bar and grill that some of her co-workers had been raving about. A few of them had tried to get her to go with them but, conscious of the strong chance she had of making junior partner within a few years, she had chosen instead to put that time to use at work.

Switching on the stereo as she pulled out of the parking lot, she wanted to try something besides her normal soft jazz. Switching the stations until she found one playing a familiar tune, she felt her mood lightening as the 80's music washed over her. She used to love Genesis, but somewhere along the way, she had forgotten that.

Invigorated for the first time in a while, she was tapping her fingers against the steering wheel when red lights started flashing in her rearview mirror. Glancing down at her speedometer, she cursed as she saw that she was going fifteen miles over the speed limit. She pulled over to the side of the road, cut the engine, and waited for the cop to stroll up to her window.

"License and registration, please."

At the deep voice, Nicole felt an unexpected shiver. Her nerve endings stood up and took notice. There was something achingly familiar about that voice. Something sexy that awakened her slumbering libido.

Looking up as she handed over the documents, she tried to see the man's features, but with the darkness of night and the wide brim on his hat, all she got was a glimpse of a strong jaw and the briefest dusting of stubble.

"Ms. Johannsen, are you aware you were doing forty-five in a thirty mile an hour zone, ma'am?"

Not bothering to lie her way out of it, she responded simply, "Yes, sir." Her mind raced, trying to figure out what was so familiar about the cop. When he turned and walked back to his cruiser, she caught a glimpse of his butt in her side mirror. Her pulse fluttered in response. He had the type of ass a woman, especially a sex starved one, could drool over. Tight and slightly rounded, he had enough cushion for a handful, but not enough to be flabby.

When he climbed into his car, she tried to see his features. Although there was enough light, the distance prevented her from seeing more than a hint of his cheekbone.

The view as he walked back towards her was even better. Watching until the last possible second, she licked her lips at his deliberate and powerful movements. He was leashed animal magnetism coupled with a uniform, and a deep, husky voice—the perfect combination.

It was beginning to drive her nuts, the sensation that she knew him from somewhere.

As he started writing on his pad, she glanced at his hand and didn't see a wedding ring, but that wasn't anything to judge by. Plenty of men she knew didn't wear a ring. So, he could still be a co-worker's husband.

Ripping the paper off, he crouched down beside her car and Nicole got her first good look at him. At first it didn't register, until he started talking again. "Seeing as how you helped me through all those torts, and you have a mostly clean record, I've decided to let you off with a warning."

"You're getting me off with a warning?" Horrified as soon as the words were said, Nicole slapped her hand over her mouth, only increasing her embarrassment. If she had played it cool, he might have thought he heard her wrong. But, flustered by her realization that the sexy cop was a former classmate, and secret object of more than one lust-filled night of self-pleasure, she overreacted.

Alan's chuckle sounded warm and incredibly relaxed as he handed a piece of paper through the window.

"No, Nicole, I'm letting you off with a warning. Now if you want, I can do the other after dinner some night." Instinctively grabbing the paper, she curled her fingers around it and sat in silence as he walked away. Through her open window, she could hear him whistling.

He pulled out from behind her, and with a wave took off into the night. After he had become nothing more than taillights winking in the night, she smoothed out the paper and found a note instead of the expected warning ticket.

My place. Tomorrow. 8PM.
1012 Elm Drive. And wear those reading glasses of yours.

Tossing the paper onto the passenger seat, she pulled back out onto the road and, rather than heading for the bar, decided to call it a night and headed for home. She pulled into her driveway several minutes later and sat there, mentally debating if she should take him up on the offer. If she did, what would they talk about? What if he wanted to do more than talk? What if all he wanted was a quick booty call?

It had been years since they had seen each other last, and obviously he hadn't followed through with law school if he was a cop. She found herself nonetheless intrigued. She had always wondered what kind of a lover Alan Vivanio would have made. But, she also wasn't looking for a quick orgasm or one night stand.

The fact that he had a dominant enough personality to go into law enforcement only added to his appeal. Tall, darkly good looking with a hot Italian temper, he was the perfect foil to her blonde Scandinavian looks and frosty temperament. Where she had always hesitated, he often spoke up, many times offering and defending her point on something in class.

Smiling, she reached over and picked up the paper, then climbed out of the car, heading into her lonely house. She would sleep on it and, in the morning when she was clear-headed, then she would decide if she wanted to explore what could be there, or if she wanted to stay with her status quo.

* * *

When the alarm went off the next morning, Nicole slapped at it until it fell silent. Curling into a ball under the covers, she tried to drift back to sleep, but images from last night kept teasing her consciousness. She could recall in vivid detail the pull of material across Alan's legs as he had walked toward her, and the curve of his pants where they cupped his groin and wrapped around his trim hips.

He had aged well, from what she had been able to see. There were a few new lines around his eyes, but they only added to his appeal. He had lost some of the boyish charm, and gained a ruggedness that she could only guess about.

Imagining how his hands would feel, no longer smooth as a baby's butt, but calloused and rough, sent a shiver down her spine. Stretching out her legs, she rolled onto her back and lightly caressed her stomach through her nightgown. As the silk brushed across her nipples and caught for a brief moment on the hard nubs, she trembled. Tiny sparks ignited within her pussy, as the desire to be filled washed over her.

Closing her eyes, she could see Alan rising over her, his hands gripping hers, holding them immobile over her head as his mouth plundered hers. His tongue would thrust past her lips, claiming her mouth as his.

Sliding her hands up to cup her breasts, she stroked the silk over the straining beads of her nipples as she imagined the rough rasp of his tongue, lapping at them. Then his hands would release hers, but a demanding glare would hold her immobile. She'd lay there submissively as he learned her body, slowly gliding his tongue and lips over her shoulders and neck, down to her breasts, and further still over her stomach and down to her aching core.

With a whimper, she followed the path of her fantasy lover with her hand, stroking along her belly, lightly caressing her inner thighs before pulling the material up and slipping a hand into her panties.

Stroking the wet flesh of her clit, she slid her fingers down past her moist lips and into her pussy. Lightly, her fingernails scraped against her inner walls as she thrust them deep, pumping it in and out of her core. She rocked her hips as she imagined the weight of her lover pressing her down into the mattress.

With her other hand, she caressed her breasts through the soft cloth of her nightgown, imagining it was a dress instead. She pinched her nipple, rolling it slowly between her fingers as she pictured Alan's teeth nipping as he slowly stroked in and out of her body with his cock.

Giving her nipple one last pinch, she slid her hand down her body and into the waistband of her panties to join the other. With one hand pumping into her pussy, Nicole stroked her clit with the other.

The first shuddering waves of her impending orgasm made her arch against her hands. In her mind's eye, she could see the smoky look in Alan's eyes as he neared his own orgasm. His lids would be half closed, like they had been many nights when they stayed up way too late studying. But instead of exhaustion, it would be desire clouding the brown depths.

Nicole could almost feel his body over hers. His tense muscles strained against hers as he pounded her pussy with his cock, his body sliding and brushing, grinding and sweating. Arching her hips, she pinched her clit between her thumb and forefinger as she thrust her fingers hard, rotating them as they slipped past her lips. With a soft whimper she climaxed, her cream quickly soaking into the material of her panties.

Gasping for breath, she continued to plunge her fingers in an imitation of her fantasy lover's thrusts, working her clit as she rode the wave of her orgasm, drawing it out as long as she could.

Reality was slow to return, but as it did a sense of loneliness followed quickly on its heels. Opening her eyes, she turned her head on her pillow and glanced at Alan's note on her nightstand. She reached out and grabbed it, her fingers still moist with her juices. Rubbing her thumb over his instructions, she made up her mind.

* * *

As Nicole had expected, by seven-thirty she was running behind. Her salon had managed to squeeze her in for a quick cut and style, she managed to shave her legs without cutting herself, and she found a dress she could live with. But she was having absolutely no luck with Alan's one request—the glasses.

She had gone through several boxes of saved items and was beginning to despair that she had tossed them out a year earlier when she switched to contacts. Just as she was digging in her tax information box on a lark, she found them.

Triumphant, she slipped them on and looked in the mirror. The moment her gaze met her own in the reflective glass, a colony of butterflies took up residence in her stomach. Sorely out of practice at the whole seduction thing, she pulled at the hem of her dress and glanced at the clock.

Red numbers glared back at her. Seven thirty-four. if she was going to make it to the address Alan had given her by eight, she had to hurry. There wasn't time to debate if another outfit would be better, or if what she was wearing would send the wrong signals. In fact, there wasn't time to do anything more than grab her purse and keys, lock the door, and head out.

Her hand shook as she tried to insert her key into the ignition, and for a moment she almost backed out. But, the possibility of ending the evening in Alan's arms rather than alone in her bed steadied her nerves. Backing the car out of her driveway, she set out, and before she knew it she was pulling onto the road in front of his house. A sudden case of nerves had her driving past his house and circling around the block. When she pulled back around, Alan was standing on his porch, leaning against the wood column, watching her. Taking a deep breath, she pulled into the driveway and killed the engine.

Her hands shook even more as she tossed her keys in her purse and climbed out. She headed up the walkway, conscious of Alan's gaze following her movements. As she climbed onto the porch, she saw him push away from the column.

The moment she reached the top of the steps, she was pulled into his arms. Before she had time to decide if she wanted to protest, his lips were covering hers, right there in front of anyone who might be watching, and devoured her mouth. Nicole felt her knees give out, and she feared that at any moment she would slide to the ground at his feet.

His hands, firm and warm against her hips, were the only things keeping her upright as his tongue rubbed against hers. Clutching at his shoulders, she leaned into the kiss, and followed as he moved to pull back.

As his lips left hers, she dropped her head to lie against his chest, breathing heavily and feeling like she had just run a sprint-- in heels--with a rabid dog chasing her.

"Alan, I--"

He tipped her face up and brushed a soft kiss against her lips. "No regrets. I'm done wondering, and waiting, and torturing myself with what ifs from the past." His fingertips brushed against her cheek and down the column of her throat to her shoulder and--slowly, achingly tender--down her arm where they curled around her wrist. He stepped back into his house, pulling her with him. The decade melted away as his dimples flashed with his smile, taking her breath away.

His place was lovely, from the warm inviting colors of the furniture and rugs to the stark photos adorning the walls. Everything had obviously been chosen with care, including the candelabra that held lit candles on the coffee table.

Large pillows had been arranged on the floor on either side of the glass topped table, and the aroma of oriental food filled the air. Nicole could remember many evenings spent studying with him over Chinese food at one of the local restaurants. She was surprised he remembered as well. As she allowed him to draw her to the table, the evening began to take on a surreal feeling.

While they ate, they talked about anything and everything. Why he had dropped out of law school and joined the police force, what her hopes and dreams were for her career. His failed marriage, and her near brush with matrimony that had ended with the knowledge her fiancée was doing more than dictating to his secretary. Even about her failure as a pet owner.

And she laughed. More than she could remember doing in a long time. The last time she had enjoyed such a simple date had been years before. Most of the men she had found time to go out with recently had been higher maintenance than she was.

As the evening progressed, she found herself reaching out to caress his hand when she made a point, or his foot would brush against her leg as he shifted on his side of the coffee table. Each touch, each accidentally purposeful brush of their bodies, increased the desire he had ignited on the porch, until she was ready to scream at him to take her and finish what he had started.

But for some reason he seemed content to wait, to tease her a little more.

She had just taken a sip of her wine after swallowing her last bite of sweet and sour chicken when he stood and held out his hand. "Dance with me," he commanded, his tone no-nonsense. Rather than bristling at his highhandedness like she would have with any other man, she found herself placing her hand in his and allowing him to pull her up.

"There's no music."

With a quick grin, he crossed the room and turned on the stereo. Moments later soft strains of music filled the room. "Now there is."

He took her into his arms, pressing her tight against his muscular frame. The fire inside her turned into a raging inferno. Moving where he guided, she was achingly aware of the glide of his thigh between her legs, the brush of his groin against her hip, the tight press of his chest against her breasts.

Laying her head on his shoulder, she pressed a soft kiss against his neck, just above the collar of his shirt. When he shuddered, she grew bolder and nipped at the slightly salty flesh, her tongue following to lap at the sting she knew she caused.

His hands slid from her back down to her ass, cupping her and pressing her tighter against his body. Emboldened, she ran her hands up and down his chest, pausing occasionally to undo a button and spread the material for her lips to caress. All the while, he slowly worked her dress up until his hands cupped her bare ass, stroking over the thong that parted her cheeks.

With a groan, he lifted her against him and she wrapped her legs around his waist, continuing to kiss his chest and shoulders as he walked down the hallway to his bedroom. They fell to the bed, and his lips claimed hers.

In the back of her mind, Nicole was shocked at her wanton behavior. Even though she had known him in college, ten years had passed. She had no clue what kind of man Alan had become. But the way he was making her feel pushed the logical part of her mind aside. A creature of pure passion rose to the surface, demanding more of his touch.

As he settled into the valley of her thighs, his groin moved against hers, generating such a delicious friction she could feel the lace of her thong growing damp with her cream. She finished unbuttoning his shirt and slipped it from his shoulders.

His hands clasped hers and pulled them over her head. "Grab the headboard," he whispered against her lips. As her fingers curled around the metal rungs he moved down her body, his breath hot enough to sear her through the thin dress. "Don't let go, no matter what."

Alan continued his downward path, until he rested at her feet. Picking up one, he cupped her ankle and pulled off her shoe. Tossing it aside, he pressed a kiss to her instep and moved up her thigh until he reached the top of her stocking. Unsnapping the garter clasp, he rolled the gossamer material down, baring her skin inch by inch, kissing all along her exposed flesh until he reached her foot again.

He pressed another kiss on her foot before dropping it to rest on the bed. Picking up her other foot, he repeated the process until her legs were bare. Knees bent, feet planted firmly on the bed more than shoulders width apart, her pussy was almost bared, except for a thin strip of lace and material covering her lips.

"I've pictured you like this for years," he said as his gaze met hers. His eyelids were half-closed, giving him a sleepy appearance, but there was nothing sleepy about his voice. Rough and hoarse with passion, his tone was like whiskey.

"You have?"

She had often fantasized about that, that after their study sessions he would head back to his place and stroke himself, imagining it was her hand caressing him. Normally it would take three fingers buried to the hilt in her pussy to fulfill her, as she'd close her eyes and picture him standing over her, his firm hands stroking his cock as he watched her masturbate.

"Yes."

She wanted to ask if she had been as much of an obsession to him as he had been to her during college, until time slowly diminished the memories, until she had forgotten all about him the last few years. Only to have that obsession renewed with the flashing of his lights in her rearview mirror.

"I almost failed the final, because of you."

"How so?"

He smiled and said, "I was so wrapped up in watching your lips wrapped around your pencil as you worked your way through the questions, I could hardly concentrate. Did you know you did that?"

Nicole shook her head. She hadn't known she sucked on her pencil, but given that her own mind had been flirting with images of sucking him off after the final, a reward for all their hard work, it wasn't surprising.

"You did. Sitting there, so perfectly untouchable with your glasses, and prim hair. Most of the guys didn't even know you existed—"

How well she remembered that part. Plain and shy, she had quickly adopted an 'ice queen' reputation to mask the hurt of not being asked out. While all her dorm-mates were out partying and enjoying life, she had been at home with her books, studying and determined to make something of herself.

"But I knew there was more to you than the icy attitude," he continued, unaware of her thoughts. "I'd watch you as we studied, and sometimes your eyes would go all glassy, your breath would catch, and I would wonder what you were thinking about. My dick would be hard, aching to rub against you, and then you would snap back to reality, and go on like nothing had happened."

Nicole started to let go of the headboard, wanting to pull him against her, but his eyes caught the movement and his gaze locked on hers, holding her immobile. He moved up between her upraised thighs and glided his hands up her body. He grasped the waist of her thong and slid it down, baring her pouting sex to the air. Sliding up further, he pressed the hard length of his frame into her body as he unhooked the strap of her dress. As he worked it down her body, she wiggled and arched, helping him all she could while still holding on to the headboard.

"The most frustrating moment of all was when class was over, and I started to ask you out, but Bill King beat me to it."

Nicole closed her eyes at the memory--what a mistake that had been. Although they hadn't worked out, he had introduced her to his cousin, who had invited her to the party where she met her former fiancée.

If only she had said no, and Alan had asked her out.

"And I watched you blossom with him, your skin glowing at the attention he showered on you, and I called myself all kinds of a fool. I let you go...because I had to. Slowly, I forgot. Or so I thought." As he talked, he caressed her body, running those roughened hands over her smooth flesh. Her breath hitched as his palms scraped over her nipples then drifted away. "Until I saw your car zipping down the road, and I ran your plate. Looking at you, sitting there so perfect and calm, honest to a fault, not even trying to worm your way out of a ticket, and I remembered all those nights we spent studying. I knew I couldn't let the opportunity slip away again."

His dipped his head and pressed a kiss against her belly button, then slipped lower. As he settled on his stomach between her thighs, his breath warm on her inner thighs, Nicole would have given anything to go back ten years before, to have discovered this moment with him then. But, knowing her younger self, she probably wouldn't have appreciated it as much as she did now, with years of lukewarm passion sprinkled with hot blasts that fizzled almost as soon as they started.

"There's so much I want to do to you, one night will never be enough." With that he dipped his head and stroked his tongue along the seam of her pussy. Like a flower unfurling for the morning sun, her pussy lips parted, welcoming the velvet heat of his tongue into her depths. He lapped and licked along her clit and the slick inner walls of her core, until she was gasping and twisting on the bed, panting and begging for more.

"You like that?" he tormented, running a fingertip along her slick skin. "Does this feel good?"

"Yes," she panted, her fingers tightening on the metal above her head.

"Tell me what you want, Nicole."

"I want you. To fuck me."

"How?" he taunted. "With my fingers, like this?"

He thrust two fingers deep within her pussy, and Nicole moaned in response. Her pussy clamped down, trying to stop the gradual withdrawal. "Is this what you want?"

"No," she gasped. She could hear the frustration lacing her words.

"What then? You have to say it, Nicole. I have to know this is what you want."

"With your dick, Alan, I want to feel your dick inside of me, fucking me!" she wailed. As the words poured forth, it felt like a wall had come crumbling down within her. "Fuck me, Alan, make me come."

Years of repressed desires, of holding herself back, were gone in that moment.

His eyes gleamed with predatory pride as he leaned over her, pulling a condom out of a drawer on the bedside table. Unzipping his pants, he quickly sheathed himself and settled between her thighs.

But unlike how she had hoped, he slowly stroked his cock against her pussy lips, barely dipping into her core before pulling back. "Alan," she whimpered.

"So prim and proper, so contained all the time," he whispered against her lips. "I always knew there was more to you that was hidden, waiting to be unleashed." Without warning, he thrust hard, sliding more than halfway in. "Do you want it soft and slow?"

Nicole looked into his eyes and saw a warmth there she hadn't seen in any of her former lovers' eyes. It was as if he was looking into her soul. "No," he answered for her, "I don't think so. You want it hard, and maybe a little rough. You want to walk out of here and know that you've been fucked."

Her eyes widened, then closed as he slammed down on her. She could feel her teeth snap together at the force. Tightening her hold on the headboard, she wrapped her legs around his waist and gripped him as tightly as she could. He pumped his hips, driving his cock so deep inside that she felt him filling her.

One of his hands cupped her ass, holding her almost immobile while the other slipped between them, and his fingers danced along her clit while he rotated and thrust his hips, creating such a delicious friction. It was so delicious that she wanted to cry and scream at the same time.

Gasping, she fought for breath as he settled into a hard and fast rhythm, the headboard beating its protest against the wall. She held onto the metal rungs as if they were the edge of a lifeboat and she was stranded in the middle of the ocean. She rode the crest and ebb of her passion as he worked them both higher and higher until, with a soft scream, she climaxed. Ripples of pleasure arced through her, drowning out everything except for the feel of his body against hers, the rough glide of his pants against her bare legs.

Even the feel of his zipper scratching at the tender skin of her inner thighs increased the sensations, until she swirled so high, her body clenched so tight, that the world went dark.

As consciousness returned, she stretched and found her hands still grasping onto the headboard. Alan's hands covered her wrists, and together they pried her stiff fingers from the metal. He pressed a soft kiss against each finger as her eyes flickered open and focus slowly returned.

He was stretched out beside her, his pants still undone, his cock lying soft against the dark material.

"I blacked out," she murmured, surprised that it had happened. Normally orgasms were nice, but never mind-blowing. Even with her battery-operated boyfriend, she hadn't experienced such a rush of adrenalin.

"Mmm, I know." Rather than the self-satisfaction she would have expected in his voice, she heard only tenderness that made her heart ache. "Shakespeare wrote of such things, a petite mort, or little death. It's poetic on paper, but more delicious to actually witness."

Rolling over, she curled up against his chest and pressed a soft kiss over his still racing heart. Despite his nonchalance, he was just as affected. She had a good idea why he was acting like he wasn't-- for her.

"Has that happened before?"

Alan brushed his lips over her hair before answering. "No."

Nicole grinned as a wicked idea started to take root. "It could have been just a reaction to years of abstinence."

"Possibly." She could hear the smile in his voice, and knew he had some idea where she was heading. Trailing her hand down his chest to the hard lines of his stomach, and down to his groin, she found his cock stirring to life.

Before her fingers could close over him, she found herself pinned on her back.

"So, we'll change the pace and take it nice and slow this time, just to be sure."

* * *

The next morning, Nicole woke slowly. A delicious feeling of warmth surrounded her. Feeling nature's demanding call, she reluctantly rolled over, only to find herself held immobile by a weight surrounding her waist. Her eyes flared open to find Alan staring down at her, lids half closed with sleep.

"Morning," he whispered, his warm breath brushing over her cheek.

Feeling utterly shy, she managed to whisper back a somewhat respectable "hi." Years before she used to fall asleep wishing she was in his arms, and she'd wake up wanting to be held by him. Now that it had actually happened, she was at a loss what to say.

Opening her mouth to tell him what a great time she had had the night before, she managed to blurt out, "I have to use the restroom" instead.

Alan's warm chuckle filled the room as he lifted his arms so she could climb out of bed. Feeling sudden warmth in her chest, she knew she had to be blushing beet red. Grabbing the edge of the sheet, she wrapped it around her in an attempt of modesty as she hurried to the bathroom.

After taking care of her morning ritual, she leaned over his sink and turned on the water. Splashing cool water on her face did nothing to remove the blush she knew would stay there for a while.

Nicole knew she couldn't stay in Alan's bathroom forever. Deciding to brave it out, she opened the door and was confronted by a very naked Alan standing on the other side of the door. Sometime in the night, he had managed to pull the covers over them, but they must have kicked the blanket to the floor. When she had wrapped up in the sheet, she hadn't thought that it might have been all that was covering Alan.

"Um, I guess you need to use the bathroom, too, huh?"

"Nope. Ran down the hall to the other bathroom while you were in there."

Rather than shift to the side and let her pass, he stepped forward, and reflexively she stepped back. "I want you to know that last night wasn't normal for me," she said, more for herself than him.

A quick smile creased his lips moments before he leaned down and kissed her, stealing her breath. The sheet dropped to the floor as she grabbed on to his shoulders for support as her knees threatened to give out.

When he pulled back, Nicole was certain she was going to fall flat on her face if he let go.

"Last night wasn't normal for me, either. And for the record, I wasn't looking for a fling."

Nicole gazed into his deep brown eyes, searching for the truth of his words. As much as she wanted to believe them, they echoed too closely her own wishes for her to be certain she hadn't heard him wrong.

"Let's take it one day at a time, and see what happens."

After a moment's hesitation, Nicole nodded.

"Good. Let's have a quick shower and we'll swing by your place for a change of clothes and go somewhere for breakfast and just talk."

Nicole slowly stroked her hand down his chest, thrilled that she could touch him as much as she wanted to, exploring the changes ten years had made to his general build. Alan's groan caused her to lose focus in her task and find him staring down at her, a heated look in his eyes. Trailing her hand just a bit lower, she brushed against the hardness of his cock.

"Lunch is good, too," he growled.

Nicole's embarrassed laugh was smothered by his lips as he kissed her again and guided her further into the bathroom for a not so quick shower.

* * *

Author's Note:

Several of the stories in this book touch on delicate topics.

In WILLED TO LOVE, a miscarriage almost tore a family apart. Regardless of how supportive a family is, the loss of a child (at any age) is devastating. If you have suffered such a loss, please - seek professional assistance if you find yourself needing it. Don't try to deal with such a tragic event alone.

DIGGIN' UP BONES deals with rape. It was not my intent to sensationalize such a horrendous attack, but rather to show the courage and strength of human will in recovering and moving past the attack. Rape is about power - and by not letting it control you, the victim takes back some of that power.

If you have been the victim of rape - please, even if you feel you can't report it - talk to someone. Don't try to go through it all alone. Talk to a friend, a therapist, or even a counselor on a 1-800 help line. One number in the US is the National Sexual Assault Hotline - 1.800.656.HOPE If you live outside of the US, a search online should yield results.

To all the survivors out there - keep living. Don't give up, and don't give the bastard who attacked you any more power over you.

* * *

ABOUT THE AUTHOR

Born to ride on the back of dragons, to journey among the stars in a ship traveling faster than light, or to dance the night away in the arms of a mysterious vampire, Michelle Houston willingly shares the worlds in her mind in an effort to bring them to life.

Writing everything from short and sweet stories, to hot and spicy tales of kink, from contemporary tales of erotic romance to erotica romances featuring Greek gods, vampires and were-creatures, she has crossed sexualities and has gone wherever her mental muse has guided her, a journey she has never regretted.

As for the more mundane details: Michelle is a Sagittarius, born in the Chinese zodiac Year of the Horse. She currently resides in the Midwest US with her husband and daughter. Michelle has a love of the natural world around us (except for insects, spiders, snakes, scorpions, and she reserves the right to add more at any time). She's one of those people that actually liked Biology in High School, and enjoys learning about all things science.

In other words, she is an ordinary woman with an imagination that is only held in bounds by how fast she can type.

You can find out more about Michelle Houston on her author website at: www.michellehouston.com